# IN THE
# EXILE ZONE

**CALUMET
EDITIONS**

Minneapolis

First Edition August 2024
*In the Exile Zone* © 2024 by George Rabasa.
All rights reserved.

10 9 8 7 6 5 4 3 2 1
ISBN: 978-1-962834-25-4

Cover and book design by Gary Lindberg

# IN THE EXILE ZONE

## SHORT STORIES

## GEORGE RABASA

**CALUMET EDITIONS**
Minneapolis

Grateful acknowledgement is given to the magazines that published the following stories:

"Feast" - *Eclipse*

"For the Solitary Soul" – *South Carolina Review,* The MacGuffin

"The Beautiful Wife" – *Glimmer Train Stories*

"Three Incidents in the Early Life of El Perro" – *Atlanta Review*

"Yolanda by Day" – *American Literary Review*

"Fallen Coconuts and Dead Fish" – *Green Hills Literary Lantern*

"The Relic" – *Licking River Review*

"The Unmasking of El Santo" – Walker Art Center (exhibition catalogue)

"Ask Senor Tototl" – *Hayden's Ferry*

In memory of Juanita Garciagodoy

# Table of Contents

# Also by George Rabasa

NOVELS

*Floating Kingdom*

*The Cleansing*

*The Wonder Singer*

*Miss Entropia and the Adam Bomb*

*Undressing Lavinia*

SHORT STORIES

*Glass Houses*

# A Boy from Brazil Kills
# the Old Man

They took the table next to ours at the famed Set Portes Restaurant in Barcelona. The man, comfortable in the generous folds of his white silk shirt, open to the third button to show off the thick links of a gold chain over his hairless chest, maneuvered his ample hips behind the table by holding on to the shoulder of his companion. The youth seemed ill at ease and was heading for the opposite seat, when the man pulled him by the wrist to sit beside him. The youth gave me a shy smile, his teeth and eyes glinting out of a very black face, skin so smooth it looked polished.

Being many years older than my girlfriend, I identified with the awkwardness of their pairing.

Kayla had made a reservation at Set Portes just that morning. I challenged her to pick a place, no matter how expensive, for a special dinner during our brief European getaway. We'd scored a choice booth under a plaque that identified the famous patrons who had dined at that very spot—Gerard Depardieu, Diego Rivera, Principe (now *Rey*) Felipe. I had hoped to impress Kayla because I sensed our thing was on borrowed time at the end of a pleasant four years. I saw myself as a fifty-something bachelor adrift in bars and dance clubs, redolent of musky cologne, a spiky haircut and discrete facial stubble, handing out my business card like a tout. I needed to extend the lease.

I could count on Kayla doing her habitual eye roll at the pretensions of the Set Portes with their thin crystal and thick silver. We studied the menu, pausing at prices and lingering over the world-famous paellas, skipping the offerings of rabbit and pigeon and pork. We were there for paella, in a kind of pilgrimage and celebration of our first trip to Barcelona when our love was new and mysterious. It would be the vegetarian for Kayla, and for me the black rice brimming with calamari in their ink.

Kayla lowered the leather-bound book of the restaurant's offerings and stole a sideways glance toward the adjacent table. The old man, who was sitting quite close, might have noticed. He put his own menu down on the table and, ignoring Kayla, turned to me with a smile.

"Pardon the intrusion," he said. "You have dined here before?"

Kayla continued pondering our options. She found it annoying that I chatted with strangers. Especially when she was giving me the morose treatment that had started our day.

"Oh yes. Last time four years ago."

"Was the paella delicious then?"

"Excellent." I tried to bring Kayla into the conversation, "Right, babe?" She acknowledged me with a nod.

"I haven't been here since 1996," he said. "I remember that it needed salt. Too bland." He then said his name was Clarence and that he liked all food, as long as it was properly salted. And that he thought Kayla and I made a charming couple.

"Well, the arroz negro is not bland."

"Gilberto would enjoy that. He's from Brazil and they like seafood. But no matter. I will order for him a paella with chorizo and blood sausage." He added with a giggle, "He will find it revolting."

I felt a twinge of sympathy for him, he being at the mercy of his overpowering host. "Habla usted español?" I said, and he responded with an even broader smile.

"Portuñol," he said. "Español y portugues mezclados."

The old man pursed his lips in disapproval. "I'm trying to teach him English, because we are sailing to New York tomorrow."

Kayla showed sudden interest. "You're getting on a ship in Barcelona?"

"Oh, it's not like the Queen Mary. More modest."

"How long will it take you to get to New York?"

The old man shrugged. "A few days. We have all the time in the world to enjoy the journey." He glanced at Gilberto and gave him a wink. To which the boy responded with a shy smile.

Our food arrived even while the pair beside us was still deciding. The man had ordered a bottle of expensive Priorat wine, and a glass of beer. "Gilberto is not fond of wine," the man explained. "Not part of his culture, as it is in Argentina and Chile which are more European."

"Of course, European." I gave Kayla raised eyebrows to which she responded with a nod. I liked that about us, the wordless communication, depending on a slight gesture, a glance, a cough, a pursed lip. As our time together seemed to be winding down, I found such moments reassuring.

"How long will the crossing take?" The idea of sea travel intrigued me, not a cruise but a purposeful journey, point A to point B.

"It's slow. Ten nights. No distractions. Ample time for friends to get to know each other. Eating, drinking, strolling the decks."

Kayla let out a sigh. "Sounds like a recipe for claustrophobia."

The man chose to respond with only a chuckle. One thing readily apparent with Kayla was that she did not engage in friendly debates. She knew what she knew and that was that. Fortunately, the early arrival of our food preempted further conversation. "Bon appetit," the old man said. She was able to muster a quick "Gracias," and then we became absorbed by the feast before us, black rice with pale bites of calamari for me, golden saffron with the tender palette of carrots and peas and cauliflower for her. We seldom conversed while eating. Nor did we read or watch the television above the bar. We respected the

3

food. The murmur in the restaurant, cheerful talk, and the clinking of silver on china, was like music.

Unlike us, the man kept a steady chatter even as he and his young guest ate, trying to converse with the boy, first in halting Portuguese then Spanish, and finally in an English monologue that required no response. The young man ate shyly, picking out of the paella only bites of chicken. Mr. Clarence murmured a reproach.

Gilberto nodded and speared a piece of sausage, gingerly putting it into his mouth, holding it there for a second before chewing rapidly and finally washing the mouthful down with gulps of beer. The old man clapped merrily.

Kayla and I exchanged a glance and went back to our meals with renewed enthusiasm. The food was good but suddenly we couldn't wait to finish eating and get out of there.

I had no issues with an old man paying for the companionship of a younger one. But in the case of Señor Clarence, there was such a clear disrespect for Gilberto that I felt sickened for having participated, even as an observer, in their cheerless game. A churn of nausea had me pushing back from the table.

As I walked off, Senor Clarence gave his friend a wink and the boy nodded with a smile. It occurred to me that I was subject of a brief silent communication, but I didn't dwell on the thought.

With a mumbled apology to Kayla, I rushed to the Men's Room. I locked the stall door behind me and stood over the toilet and waited for the occasional reluctant flow. I flushed for inspiration and finally standing straight, pissed out a healthy stream.

I zipped up but when I turned to open the door, there was Gilberto with a smile, as if he'd been waiting for me, standing still, hands on hips and fly undone. With his back to the main part of the restroom, all gleaming lights and brass fixtures and marble counters, his erect penis was visible only to me. This was the first time in my life that I had confronted another man's erection. I was at a loss as to how to react. Did this young guy really think we could close ourselves in a stall in a fancy restaurant and have ourselves a moment? Surely, he was not that naïve. And in any case, what had made him think that I would respond?

I looked at him and acknowledged his presence with a nod and then started to move past him. He was tall and broad shouldered, almost intimidating if it wasn't for his soft large eyes and dumb grin. He stood at the doorway to the stall, and as far as I could see past him, we were alone in the restroom. Just as I was contemplating having to push him aside, there was the slam of the door and men's voices.

"Gilberto, con permiso, vuelvo a la mesa," I said loudly. Never before had my high school Spanish served me so well. It got his attention; he stepped aside and then ducked into the stall as I exited.

I stood at the sink, splashing water on my face and slicking down my hair, letting my breath return to normal. A man washing his hands beside me hardly glanced my way. From the stall behind me, Gilberto's shoes were now pointing forward. All was back to normal in the world of the "Caballeros."

I'd been gone for several minutes, but Kayla hardly gave me a look. Mr Clarence did fix me with an arched eyebrow, which I ignored. His marshmallow face, dominated by a protuberant nose, small squinty eyes, and thick lips flecked at the edges with spittle, held a schoolboy meanness.

I devoured the last forkfuls of paella and asked for the check. No coffee, no dessert, no after-dinner cordial, gracias. Kayla seemed startled by my haste, but without a word she quaffed the last of the wine. I pushed my chair back as Gilberto was returning from the Caballeros. His bemused expression made me wonder if he had made a friend after our encounter. I left a handful of euros on the table and we, with barely a nod to Clarence and Gilberto, were out of there.

We paused outside on the canopied passageway to regain our bearings. "We need to go back to Set Portes soon," Kayla sighed. "I hardly enjoyed the meal sitting next to that pair."

"An odd couple."

"Señor Clarence," she laughed. "Creepy."

"And Gilberto."

"Poor kid."

"Yeah. Poor. He followed me into the men's room and showed me his penis."

"Just like that?"

"I started to leave the stall and there I was, facing a hardon."

"What did you say?"

"Nothing that I recall. I might have nodded as if to say, yeah, I see it and it is indeed a handsome tool you have."

"I knew something like that was going on," she said. "I was wondering if you would tell me."

"How did you know?"

"The man turned to Gilberto and gave him a look."

"What do you mean, a look?"

"You know, a *look* look. But the boy didn't react until the man gave his shoulder a nudge."

\* \* \*

Outside, under a pure blue autumn sky, Kayla and I strode down the Rambla. Our two dining neighbors had proved so stifling that we laughed at the relief of being out of their presence. We ended at a table right on the boulevard with a couple of cortados, thick and strong with just the right drizzle of milk. Before us, the street theater surged with energy. The Mad Hatter offered us tea. A team of hide-the-bean touts tempted us to win a few pesetas. Before us a parade of handsome boys and girls, pilgrims with tanned legs and flat bellies, navigated the currents of the boulevard toward Columbus with his finger pointing to beyond the sea.

Earlier that day, we had awoken to a noisy morning on Passeig de Gracia outside our room. I had wanted to make love, but I knew to be considerate of Kayla's slow emergence into wakefulness. I brushed my teeth and rubbed the stubble on my face and sniffed my armpits. Deeming my hygiene acceptable, I crawled back inside the covers.

"I need coffee," she said, shuffling out of reach.

I tugged at her shoulder. "Play now? Then breakfast."

"So, I fuck for food now?"

"Maybe for coffee?" I started to laugh but then I realized that she was not finding any humor in my attempts. I rolled away and lay on my back, eyes shut to the sunlight burning through the gauzy curtain. Still, I made no attempt to get dressed for breakfast or even call room service. I had a tough time with rejection after four years of a happy relationship, since our first stabs at connection the evening she picked me up while driving an Uber shift.

"Hi, I'm Kayla and you're Brandon, right?"

"Nice car," I said as I got into the front seat of a new Prius. I liked to compliment the Uber drivers on their rides. They needed the reinforcement after getting in debt buying a late-model car that the service would approve.

"Where to, Mr Brandon?"

"Ordway."

"What are you seeing?"

"Opera. Don Giovanni. By Mozart, the composer."

"As opposed to Jake Mozart the linebacker or Suzy Mozart the movie star?"

"I didn't mean to patronize."

"I haven't heard Don Giovanni. I've heard *of* him."

"One the worst men in the world. He dies at the end and goes to hell."

"Seems like wishful thinking."

"Yes, but there is the gorgeous music too."

"That explains you all dressed up for the occasion."

She had noted my appearance, so I felt free to stare at her skirt, which rode up above her knees and a sleeveless top in some silky fabric in acqua green with a trim of embroidered flowers at the neckline that showed off the contour of her breasts, evidence that she had dressed for the occasion as well. I imagine she was aware that I was looking at

7

her insistently, but she concentrated on driving, her small size, which I guessed was just over five feet, forcing her to sit straight and stare through horn rimmed glasses.

"Unfortunately, my girlfriend bailed at the last minute."

"Not nice of her."

"A not very nice migraine." Then I paused for a moment as I decided to act on impulse. "You could park and use her ticket."

"Wow, that would be *so* unprofessional." She turned for the road to flash me a radiant smile. I fell in love with Kayla.

\*\*\*

She was slow to leave the concert hall even after the artists had taken their curtain calls and the crowd had thinned out. I started to stand but she took my hand and pulled me back down to the chair. "Better than rock n' roll," she exclaimed. The sextet ensemble at the end when Giovanni is sent to hell was an onslaught of voices bouncing and somersaulting and spinning off each other.

As we left the theatre, I offered to summon an Uber but she insisted that the ride was on her. I talked her into a drink. Café Wilde was mostly deserted, and we got a quiet booth toward the back. I ordered cava and gazed at her through the bubbles in the glass. We ended up sharing a bottle of Freixenet and when Wilde declared last call, I convinced her that she was too buzzed to drive.

That's how things started between Kayla and me. I couldn't have written a better script. Over the course of the night, she admitted to a boyfriend who was handsome and boring, the one thing she could not forgive. The fuck buddy, as I called him in my mind, was a day trader who spent his waking hours on the MacPro clicking buys and sells with mechanical abandon. She liked that he was mostly unavailable outside his apartment, which gave her the flexibility to hang out with her women friends, mainly for dancing and music.

"So, he is mostly using you."

She shrugged. "We use each other."

"I will not use you," I said as we lay side by side in the early morning. "And you can take me for granted."

"Ha! You don't know what you're getting into."

And so began my Kayla mission, a gradual meddling with her unschooled intelligence. I gave her books to read (The Bell Jar, TS Eliot's poetry, Madame Bovary) and then I read her some passages because I wanted to experience art through her eyes and ears. She made quick appraisals: Silvia Plath was a narcissist, Emma Bovary was the victim of a misogynist author, but TS Elliot was on to profound though murky things.

We went to museums, concentrating on Picasso. If she could get the great Pablo, she would move on to everything else in the 20th century. Then, gradually back in time. Art history as taught ass backwards. We listened to opera and chamber music and choral works. We watched my favorite movies. Last Tango in Paris, La Dolce Vita, The Conversation, almost anything by the Coens.

And we made love. Or rather, I made love to her. She lay back and allowed me to give her pleasure. Slowly, tenderly, or quickly as the mood hit me on a snowy afternoon or first thing in the morning. I don't think she had ever experienced a lover's generosity. When she asked what she could do for me that would excite me, I assured her that her arousal was a gift to me. I ran my hands lightly along the skin of her back and her thighs, feeling the bumps and shivers of her response, then finally the blessed wetness that swallowed me whole.

She moved into my condo after a month, just in time, too, as she was deep into uncomfortable discussions with her roommates in the once grand mansion they shared in St Paul. Whatever can be said about Kayla's self-assurance and intelligence, she was not cut out for domesticity. Money was an abstraction unless required to solve an immediate problem; she seemed to have no financial obligations beyond the leased Prius. Her Uber shifts were maddeningly unpredictable, especially on weekends when she'd be out till 3:00 harvesting drunk students from the bars. Other times, she'd sit around all day waiting for the ping that promised an airport ride, with likely surge pricing.

Our arrangement was perfect. I was creating a woman that I could be comfortable with, a malleable, eager student of the life I valued. I felt a great responsibility for my Kayla mission, which would only succeed if she herself saw value in it. That's not to say she was entirely docile. She pushed back on jazz and jalapeños and Kant. All capable of inducing headaches at the first taste. And she brought to me her generation's perspective on sex and money and the compromises that resulted in having too much of one and not enough of the other.

Things were comfortable between us until about three years into our relationship. I'm not sure what went wrong or why the arrangement that we had developed, would eventually prove to be untenable. Things were just fine, and then they weren't. I can't remember the exact moment when this became clear to me, if not immediately to Kayla.

At times during our friendship, the banter would grow caustic. She would tease me about being old and idle and rich, and I would lord over her that I was the education she had missed in art and music, political science, literature, philosophy, and other subtle and hidden ways of the world.

She liked calling me Professor. Which flattered me, even when I sensed irony. "Yes, Prof, Whatever you say, Prof, or even Forgive your stupid pupil, Professor Higgins."

"You're not stupid."

"Then, try not to make me feel that way."

"Hey. Ignorance is not stupidity."

"So knowledge is not proof of brilliance?"

Eventually, our routine wore thin. She accused me of harboring a collection of facts that I wielded when I needed an edge. Suddenly, I was to feel embarrassed that I knew the details of the Mexican revolution or the truth about the poisonous datura or foxglove flowers. She called me a breathing set of Trivial Pursuit. I could not apologize for reading widely and remembering interesting nuggets. I did apologize for showing off, but not sincerely enough because she continued to sulk.

She had been sulking our first day in Barcelona, withdrawing into a passive indifference. Nothing that I said amused or interested or provoked her. And when I pushed for us to have sex, she resisted.

"You don't get to fuck me on demand because you pay the bills."

"No. Because I know we will both experience pleasure. And because sex makes our life together happier."

"You can say the same thing for breakfast."

In the end, we made love first. I knew that I had been right to insist. We enjoyed ourselves. I, maybe more than her.

Then for breakfast, the café con leche and croissants with the tips dipped in dark chocolate. A perfect morning, I claimed. As in other occasions when I had somehow prevailed on her sexual indifference, I tried to chat my way back into a good place in her mind. The modernist, medieval, cubist wonders all around us. And the hipness of modern-day Barcelona, now the coolest city in Europe.

That was when we decided to have lunch at Set Portes. Surely, paella and a good wine would set things aright.

However, we ended up sitting beside the old man and the Brazilian boy.

I thought Senor Clarence and young Gilberto had been left behind when they appeared within the river of humanity that strode the Rambla. Kayla spotted them first and dug her elbow into my side to get my attention. The old man. trying to hold himself erect, walked unsteadily with a lumbering gait, moving slowly with the Brazilian boy offering his arm. Kayla and I were caught up in the throng, several steps behind them. Even in the midst of the crowd, the old man towered above most passersby.

It was a luminous afternoon and the sun shone on the flower stalls and the bird vendors and the souvenir stands and the sweet shops. Everything took on a seductive glow and the birds were brightly plumed and the flowers explosive in their color and the ice cream flavors rich in pastels of lavender and pink. Señor Clarence stopped to get ice cream cones, strawberry for him and dark chocolate for Gilberto. They sat on a sunny bench, where they could enjoy their treats and watch the passersby. Kayla and I hung several steps back and browsed among the cages of a bird seller, his flock chirping excitedly as we peered into their delicate little jails. It was hard to tell whether they viewed us as threats or expected us to be adopted in the tradition of puppies and orphans.

From our vantage point we could see the pair were in animated conversation. Mostly the old man scolding, head bobbing, hand occasionally raising as if to threaten a slap. During such a move the man's scoop of ice cream rolled off the cone and landed at his feet. The young man, visibly apologetic as if he'd been the one that caused the accident offered the old man his own ice cream. The man nodded and took the cone. Then, as if in retaliation, he tipped it slowly until the chocolate scoop rolled to the ground. They sat stiffly, shoulders lightly touching, as they watched how the strawberry and chocolate balls softened and melded into a single puddle.

After a few minutes, when the two flavors had run together in the afternoon swelter, Clarence said something, and Gilberto nodded. He stood in front of the older man and offered him his arm. Sitting had stiffened the man's movements, and he pulled himself up with Gilberto's help.

Their walk together became a slow trudge and the old man was hardly able to take steps of a few inches at a time. And yet young Gilberto shuffled along with him patiently. They eventually reached the end of the Rambla, where Passeig de Gracia and Pelai converged at the Plaça Catalunya circle in a sudden traffic cluster of cars and bikes and motorcycles and buses competing to get free.

The two were waiting at the edge of the boulevard for a Walk signal to allow them to walk across the avenue. Gilberto, standing very close to the old man, massaged his back with long caresses, finally sliding his hand down to give his buttocks a squeeze. Kayla and I, still unseen, were only a few feet from them. We were amused by the boy's bold move, until we saw that with a firm push at Señor Clarence's ass, Gilberto had sent him falling face down into the path of rushing traffic. Kayla gasped and clutched my hand, digging in her nails in silent anguish. Screams sounded from all around us as the old man was struck head-on by a sightseeing bus manned by a guide trumpeting the glories of Barcelona. With a high-pitched wail Gilberto rushed into the street, halting traffic with more yells and waving arms. "Accidente!" he moaned. "Ayuda por favor." And then, he glanced back at us as if he'd known all along that we were close behind him. His gaze locked onto Kayla's and, in that instant, a look of understanding flashed between them.

# The Unmasking of El Santo

Benito Segura feels the weight of tradition. Before Gorgeous George or Jesse Ventura or The Rock or Stone Cold Steve Austin, there was El Santo. Benito owns the look: silver Speedo trunks over pearly gray tights; high-top sneakers bright with metallic polish. He unfurls the satin cape in the mirror, his brown hairless chest glistening with baby oil, snaking muscles along the arms and shoulders, belly sucked into the waistband. El Santo keeps himself buff. The shiny satin mask—with the slits for eyes, like a wildcat's, and the outline of the mouth, thick lips curling with contempt—remains unviolated. Even in this incarnation, nobody can put a lock on El Santo. The identity of the unknown paladin is still secret.

Benito waits for adventure. He knows the bad elements of the neighborhood, the boys in the gangas and the dealers in the alley. He came to St. Paul from Uruapan twenty years ago, an experienced pastry baker with the memorized recipes of conchas, corbatas, chilindrinas, cuernitos, chalupas, orejas, huesitos, cocoles, vidrios, polvorones... Now, he sits behind Panadería La Esperanza, taking a break from the rolling of dough for bolillos and teleras. A bandana keeps the flour out of his hair, but his arms are streaked with masa and his fingertips stained brown from the hot sugar. He drinks sweet coffee in the alley and hangs with the vagos, listens to their bragging, their mocking jokes, their nudging snickers when a girl walks by. He remembers their boasts. Nobody knows that at night Benito goes out as El Santo and looks for the opportunity to mess things up for the bad guys.

On this Saturday night, El Santo cruises Robert and Concord Streets, then across the river to Bloomington and Lake, riding low in a '87 Impala, stealthy around the corners like a mountain lion. Wherever trouble happens, El Santo will be there, ready to defend the weak and the old, the soft and naive, children and grandmothers, and women in tight dresses.

Action at last: Two guys in a Ford Explorer, gringuitos with yellow hair, out to score. El Santo parks in the shadows and rushes out from behind a building waving his cape. The dopers scream, *holy shit!* They get back in their car and peel out, thinking they have seen a ghost. Meanwhile, the two dealers chase El Santo until he loses them in a lightning sprint into the dark. The cabrones curse him and yell, chinga tu madre, and say if we ever find out who you are, pendejo, you will be hurting bad. Benito's heart goes haywire; he whispers a panicked appeal to the Virgen de Guadalaupe. Mother of God!

The following Monday, word of the crime busting gets around. The customers in the bakery are buzzing about El Santo, a real hero of the community. But they add sadly, whoever he is, once he is found out, he is roadkill. Benito, naked to the waist, appears from behind the ovens, wiping the sweat off his face with the edge of his long apron. He says he knows who El Santo is. Nobody believes him. Just wait and see, Benito grins. He is dying to tell.

# Ask Señor Totol

Matthew Weldon and Sarah, currently Weldon but soon to revert to Marley, had taken a break from their unhappy chore and now sat cross-legged at opposite ends of the living room. Even at rest, cheerfully attired in shorts and T-shirts, Katmandu for her, Cancún for him, they were facing the sort of change that can bring on cardiovascular agitation, malignant bumps, fiery shingles, and the aggravation of various dependencies: the Weldons were dividing their possessions into three mounds.

The largest pile, at the apex of the triangle, consisted of a dismantled sectional sofa upholstered in nubby oatmeal. A floor lamp with a fringed shade lay across two sofa sections. There was also an end table with a wrought-iron base, a hat stand without hats, a fake fichus, an old television, a brown dog. These were things that the Weldons had accumulated in their eighteen years together, but that neither wanted to keep, now that their minds had been made up. That stuff would go to Goodwill. The dog, a fat hound called Bruno, nearly as old as the marriage, but still enjoying the occasional chase of a chewed-up frisbee or a spongy tennis ball, would be a problem.

The other two stacks represented a fair division of literature and music from the sublime to the stupid, decor and gadgetry balanced for aesthetic as well as utilitarian value. And, again, old Bruno sniffing his way from one pile to the other.

Some potential for conflict remained. Awaiting fair partitioning were the various oddities the Weldons had collected in the course of their years of travel and modest adventure: a luminous chunk of amber from Moldavia, a fake jívaro shrunken head made of chicken skin but with tufts of real human hair, a fat little Bodhisattva carved out of ivory, a vial of cloudy Lourdes water, an opium pipe from Shanghai, its bowl black with tar and its stem notched with tooth marks, a clay Satan with a huge penis that jerked up and down when his tail was pulled. Among them, was the mysterious *totoltetl*, an egg-like object covered with a fine golden down that looked as if it had been laid by some exotic bird.

The Weldons had acquired the reputed healing amulet from an herbalist in the Oaxaca market, while on their honeymoon. The furry egg, which had been growing progressively more wrinkled and dustier on its shelf, had become, after nearly twenty years of curious mysteries and unexplained phenomena, too established in their lives to throw out.

"You're the one that found it at the witch doctor's stand," Sarah said, trying to hand the object to Matthew. "It's more your thing."

"I wouldn't know what to do with it now," he said. "You keep it."

"Nope, it has way too much history for me." She continued to hold it out toward him.

Mathew took the totoltetl and held it gingerly in the palm of his hand. He stroked the back of his finger against the grain of its fleece, so that the fuzz quickened as if by static electricity.

The herbalist had offered it first to Sarah. "Oh, how cute, how curious," she'd said without much enthusiasm. Matthew was more interested in the thing's healing properties. The merchant called it a totoltetl, but when asked what exactly that was, the man was vague. "Un huevo, a bird stone," he shrugged. "A special egg. Very useful."

Tucked inside a cap, a totoltetl relieves headache. In a pants pocket close to the groin, it favors potency. In a pouch hanging from a leather cord at the center of the chest, it can steady the heart's rhythms.

Sandwiched between lovers' bellies, it could heighten and prolong orgasm. He said nothing about the oracular attributes it eventually manifested.

The totoltetl was all the more mysterious because its utility was not readily apparent. It attracted attention, yet most people seemed content to admire it at a distance. "Go ahead, touch it," Matthew would laugh. "It's all fuzzy, like a newborn's head."

Now, after the other souvenirs had been separated into the two opposing piles of stuff, the totoltetl remained unclaimed, its consequence enhanced by its solitude. In the waning afternoon light, its golden fuzz seemed to ignite, the fine down aglow. Sarah was sure that the amulet was party to their escalating troubles.

*\*\**

The totoltetl had sat on the shelf, its powers untried, one night, when their best friends Iona and Stu were invited to come and cook dinner together. Iona was suddenly hammered by a fierce headache. Matthew thought that she would be the perfect subject for the totoltetl; Iona was the most rational and pragmatic of their friends, the only Ph.D. in mathematics Matthew had ever met. He was a little intimidated and secretly enamored by her. He called her Our Lady of Logic, the Queen of Calculations. Her pain would put the totoltetl to a definitive test.

"This is one of your exotic third-world finds?" Iona wrinkled her nose even though the totoltetl gave off no smell.

"Haven't you got any aspirin?" Stu asked.

"I have a hunch this could help," Matthew said. "In any case, it's totally natural medicine. Nothing to swallow, inhale or inject."

"I'd let you cut my head off, darling, if you thought it would help," said Iona.

Matthew pulled out a shaggy woolen scarf he kept rolled up in his overcoat pocket. He shook off the winter's accumulation of cough drop wrappings, cookie crumbs, and movie ticket stubs. He tied the ends of the scarf under Iona's chin so that the magic egg stood like a bump on top of her head. "Hold still," he said after a light nod threatened to send the totoltetl sliding down.

"I was trying to talk," she said.

"Talk with your head still, sweetheart," her husband said.

Iona nodded again; the egg tipped forward. She raised her hand to catch it in time. She sighed while Matthew repositioned the egg and tied the scarf more securely. "How long is this going to take?"

Matthew shrugged. "Keep still for ten minutes and see what happens."

"Fine, I'll just sit here in the dark." Keeping her head resolutely erect, she reached over to the table lamp and snapped off the light. She dismissed everyone with a wave of her fingers. "Meanwhile, somebody find me the ibuprofen."

The three friends gathered in the kitchen. They had cooked together before and they moved smoothly, basting, slicing, stirring. Stu opened a bottle of cabernet. Sarah mashed garlic for aioli.

"I'd better go check on Iona," Matthew said, after a while. The others nodded their heads without much enthusiasm. There was the unspoken expectation that she would ruin the evening's good cheer with the persistence of her pain and sour mood.

Several minutes later Matthew reentered the kitchen, gently guiding Iona ahead of him. She seemed dazed, but she was also smiling with relief.

"We have a miracle," Matthew announced. "Iona's headache has vanished."

"What took so long in there?" Sarah asked, though nobody seemed to hear.

"It was incredible," Iona nodded enthusiastically. "I felt as if a tiny hole had been drilled on top of my skull and this egg thing was sucking up the pain."

"Shows what faith will do," Sarah said.

"Faith had nothing to do with it," Iona said. "This fuzz ball worked without any help from me."

They were silent for a few moments, gazing with renewed respect at the totoltetl in Matthew's palm. Then Sarah put it back on the mantel, and said it was time to stop talking about headaches and couldn't they just sit down and have a nice dinner?

\*\*\*

For a time, the totoltetl became Matthew's magic remedy. He cured everything and everyone with it. He wrapped it around his knee when he sprained it running and was miraculously back on the road three days later. The totoltetl was rubbed across a baby's tummy to ease colic. It cured hemorrhoids while tucked into his father's back pocket.

"It has a .500 batting average," Matthew would say to diminish expectations whenever he was asked to apply the totoltetl's powers to another case of hypertension or high cholesterol. He would speak with great authority: "Reduce salt, exercise a little, sleep more, work less, quit smoking, drink moderately, pay off credit cards, avoid your mother; the totoltetl will do the rest." That got laughs.

Matthew wouldn't leave the house without taking his wondrous egg along. It helped him find parking spots, avoid traffic jams, beat blizzards. He carried it in a leather pouch, either around his neck or hanging from his car's rearview mirror. "Do your thing, Señor Totol," became a common refrain. It would go with him on business trips, to client meetings, ball games. Mostly, Matthew's luck was good. When things didn't turn out as hoped, then he would tell himself that the totoltetl knew best, that the account lost or the promotion missed were blessings in disguise.

He took a picture of it and turned it into their holiday greeting card. "May the spirit of Señor Totol dwell in your heart."

Meanwhile, it seemed that the egg had a bias against Sarah's pains. She tried it for menstrual cramps. Even with Matthew's warm hands on the egg, guiding its fuzzy path along her belly, nothing happened. When she tried using it by herself, she could swear that besides the pain persisting, a wave of anxiety would crawl like ants along her skin. In the end, she left the capricious thing on its shelf.

\*\*\*

Matthew started using the totoltetl the way some might throw the I Ching coins or read the Tarot. The egg was more direct and unambiguous, no muddled answers due to subjective interpretation or vague translation. He found that he could roll it down the floor and the totoltetl would unpredictably veer from its straight path. A right turn meant yes; left was no. Time after time, the roll of the totoltetl proved to be prophetic. Should Matthew accept Cannon & Lemke's job offer? The fuzzy egg rolled down the carpet, seemed to hesitate for a moment, wobbled in its direction, and finally hit a tight left turn: No. Minutes before he was to phone in his decision, the totoltetl had given its answer. Matthew passed up a twelve-thousand dollar raise. A couple of months later, the account he was to work on went to another agency, leaving eight people in the lurch.

The egg was building a track record: The house that the totoltetl told the Weldons to not buy collected a foot of water in the basement during the next big rainstorm. On the totoltetl's say-so, their big bold investment in Intel stock went up, up, up. Matthew became more wary of life's uncertainties. There was just no way to know logically how a trip might turn out, when to appeal for a raise or a promotion, which make of car to buy. But Señor Totol usually knew.

The totoltetl became an ally in its owner's secret life: Mathew grew idiotically in love with Iona. The feeling had grown on him after the first night he had cured her headache. He had touched her forehead and felt a rush of heat radiating to his fingers. He was sure that a tangible exchange of energy had happened between them. Whenever he consulted the totoltetl, usually in the middle of the night, when thoughts of Iona's penetrating looks and knowing smile disturbed his sleep, he would ask if the time was right for him to simply call her, ask her to lunch, make a clear move. The answer from the egg was always no: You will not make an ass of yourself.

He sinned in thought every day. Lust was only one of his transgressions. He was also guilty of deceit, covetousness, hypocrisy, selfishness, envy and sentimentality. He became the consummate liar, not only in word, but also in gesture and expression. The too-casual chuckle at one of Iona's deliciously ironic comments, the bland look after one of her perfunctory pecks on the cheek, the surreptitious ogling at the swell of a breast or the flick of her tongue. The occasional dinner parties or nights out with Stu and Iona were occasions of both torment and meager delight.

A winter night in 2015 marked the transformation of his private love for Iona. From naked devotion it evolved into grief and worry, and, finally, deep unshakable mourning. Details remained vivid. He remembered driving with Sarah to their friends' house across town under the weight of a heavy wet snowfall, blanketing the streets, muffling the sounds of traffic, creating mushy slippery tracks. It had grown dark by five, and approaching headlights were fragmented into a multitude of reflections through the falling snow. There was little sense of the road's shoulders and the progress though the whiteness was guided more by instinct and memory than any sense of proper trajectory.

He parked by barreling into the first welcoming snowbank half a block from their friends' house. Sarah carried a chocolate torte in both hands for no particular occasion, but simply for the satisfaction that the four friends were lean and fit from summer's running. The act of eating joyfully was a celebration of their virtuous life. Matthew carried a bottle of forty-dollar cabernet, which was additionally a celebration of their faith that the good times would endure. The totoltetl rested cozily inside his coat pocket.

Later when he and Sarah would compare their memory of the evening, they agreed that something was tangibly out of kilter in the way that Stu and Iona welcomed them into the porch for the removal of wet of boots and the shaking off of snowy coats and hats. Entering the stiflingly warm living room, redolent with the scents of garlic and basil, they'd noticed that Stu had greeted them too expansively, and that Iona's hands felt cold when she clasped theirs.

There seemed to be little to talk about that night. There was praise for the food. The wine's shortcomings were more emphatically expressed because of its price. They reminisced briefly about the joys of eight-dollar chianti jugs and the advantages of the uncultivated palate. They played with Stu's new espresso machine, La Combinazzione, and marveled at how it managed to make two cappuccinos simultaneously, in half the time of their previous model but with twice the hissing of steam and the groaning of its mighty pump.

There was a quiet moment then, over coffee and the spectacular chocolate confection. Iona asked Matthew if he had brought the totoltetl along. It had been a long time  since Matthew had even mentioned it, but there didn't seem to be much doubt in Iona's mind that the miracle healing object from the depths of Oaxaca was there, in Matthew's coat pocket, ready for action.

"You have a headache, Iona?" Matthew asked.

"No," she said. "A question."

"Sure," Matthew said. "Señor Totol likes questions, as long as they're simple and direct."

"It's a yes-or-no kind of question," Iona said.

"Perfect." Matthew nodded. "There's no 'maybe' in the egg's vocabulary."

Stu rose from his chair and stood behind Iona, resting his hands on her shoulders. "Let's not spoil a nice evening, darling. I don't think Matthew is up to playing parlor games."

"I don't consider the totoltetl a game," Matthew said.

"He is very serious about the old egg," Sarah added.

"I need to ask it something," Iona insisted, flashing Stu a serious look. She waited while Matthew went to the closet and withdrew the totoltetl from his coat pocket. He sat cross-legged on the carpet beside Iona, the fuzzy egg resting motionless before them. He explained about the totoltetl rolling down a smooth path and eventually turning right for yes, left for no.

"That's it?" said Iona. "Who rolls it?"

"It should be the person asking the question."

"Yes, but you're the one that's in tune with the thing."

Matthew shrugged modestly. "I have had good results with questions," he said.

"Fine. I'll ask and you roll," Iona said taking a deep breath as if to steady the tremor in her voice. "Do I ask my question out loud?"

"Well, I think the person rolling the totoltetl should be aware of the question," he said. "I don't think the totoltetl would know who was asking. In any group at any given time there must be a dozen questions hovering in our minds."

"There would be a collective energy," Matthew nodded.

"I think this is really stupid," Stu said.

Sarah watched, slouching into the cushions of a deep velvet sofa, feeling distant from the others. The oddness she had picked up in the air from the moment they had entered Stu and Iona's house was now wafting through the room like the smell of exhaust. "Dr. Matthew in action," Sarah said. Nobody reacted to her comment; she knew herself to be unimportant in whatever dynamic had arisen among the three.

Matthew picked up the totoltetl, warm and weighty now on the palm of his hand, as if the moment's tension had endowed it with more than its usual measure of power. He held it up to Iona. "Touch it when you ask the question," he said.

She waited several moments, hardly looking at the object that Matthew held within her reach. "The question is," she rested her fingers on the egg. "Is it malignant?"

"Not at all," Matthew said, holding the totoltetl up for Iona to see.

"Not that," she said impatiently. "It. The *it* that is in me. Is it or is it not, you know, benign. Or not."

There was a moment of dense, awkward silence, until Stu finally cleared his throat. "Our families don't know. The doctors don't know."

"We only know that there's something here." Iona glanced vaguely toward her left breast.

Stu nodded. "We have to be at the clinic by seven tomorrow."

Sarah took in a breath that was like a loud startled gasp to her own ears. She was relieved to be participating in this moment with some degree of invisibility. She glanced at Matthew who had grown pale. She was not surprised that he was taking the news so hard; the possibility of Iona's breasts being carved up by surgeons represented the end of something beautiful and perfect in his eyes.

"But I want to know now," Iona broke in. "At least be ready."

Stu cleared his throat again, as if every attempt at speech had to be censored. "I think we should leave it up to the doctors."

"I don't want to wake up all groggy and the first thing I learn is that my breast is gone. Do you mind? I would like some preparation." She paused as if to steel her resolve. "Matthew dear, just roll the thing, will you?"

"Okay," he nodded briskly. "Left turn is no, right is yes."

Iona touched the totoltetl, as if to feel the subtle force that emanated from its fine downy covering. "The question is," she stated formally, "is my lump malignant?"

The egg rolled down the carpet in a straight line, slowed down to a wobble, then, as if reanimated by some inner force, turned abruptly to the right. It went another two feet, then stopped with a slight rocking motion.

The group stared at the spot where the totoltetl had made its turn, as if through some collective, unspoken prayer they could coax it into reversing its course.

"Jesus," Stu whispered. "So much for that."

Sarah searched for something to say to Iona. "This thing of Matthew's, well, it's a game, isn't it," she said. "The important thing for tomorrow is to think positive. For all of us to think positive."

Matthew looked at his wife gratefully. "That's right," he said to Iona. "Positive energy is what is called for."

Iona took a deep breath. "Actually," she said. "I have another question."

"No fucking way," Stu blurted.

"I think Stu is right," Matthew said, shaking his head as if coming out of a daze.

"I'll roll it myself," Iona said. "None of you need to know what I'm asking."

Stu reached down to the floor, picked up the egg and tossed it to Matthew. "Just take the damn thing home with you, buddy. We're done playing."

"It was my idea, Stu," Iona said tersely. "It's still my idea."

"Well, you can do whatever you want, but I'm not having any part of it, and neither are our guests," Stu said. He rose as if declaring the evening over. Matthew and Sarah stood as well, waiting for Stu's cue. "I propose we fire up La Combinazzione for one more surge."

They went into the kitchen and Iona stayed in the living room. Matthew wanted to be with her, even if he didn't know what she was asking. He felt she must suddenly feel very alone with her frightening questions and the unpredictable turns of the totoltetl. He slurped the golden crema off the surface of his espresso and grew progressively more anxious as he envisioned Iona watching for the totoltetl's answer.

A few minutes later, Iona came into the silent kitchen. She looked calm. Her features had settled into a kind of ambiguity, as someone who has received bad news realizes that the effect is not as terrible as had been envisioned. She eagerly handed the totoltetl back to Matthew, giving no clue as to what the question and corresponding answer had been. She asked Stu to make her a cappuccino. He seemed glad to do something for her after his outburst. It was the perfect moment for the Weldons to say good night.

The drive home was easier because the blizzard had stopped, and the traffic had compacted the snow so that Matthew could feel the wheels under him crunching solidly along the rutted tracks. He stared ahead, feigning intense concentration.

***

Since that evening, the totoltetl had sat on the shelf, untouched, radiating a kind of knowledge which seemed best untapped. Now, the separating Weldons were done dividing their possessions, and still the totoltetl remained unclaimed. Sarah would have no part of it; it had really been Matthew's. She grew increasingly irritated now that he did not want this thing, which seemed to be begging for some resolution to its fate. There ought to be a dignified way for objects to crawl back into the cosmos after outgrowing their usefulness. Cars were traded in. Books were lent. Clothes faded into charity. Dishes broke. Friends moved on.

Matthew sat on the carpet, holding the totoltetl within the V formed by his outstretched legs. It was the first time he had touched it since the night when Iona had asked her questions. He twirled it like a top. He batted it back and forth, rolled it toward one knee, then the other.

From a sofa section, Bruno perked up his ears, stared dimly at the rolling egg, then once more rested his head back between his massive paws. He lazily followed the totoltetl's twirls and zigzags through dropping eyelids.

"I wish you wouldn't do that," Sarah said. When Matthew looked up at her, raising his eyebrows and feigning ignorance, she added, "You're making me dizzy the way you go on with the thing."

"I'll trade you the totoltetl for the red Zapotec rug."

"In your dreams."

"Señor Totol could prove useful sometime." He held up the fuzzy egg as if to tempt her. "You may one day ask it whether you should marry some other guy. It could save you big misery."

"Nothing saves us big misery," Sarah said.

"The right question and answer at an opportune time can." He gazed at her as if waiting for a response to his statement. But she neither agreed nor disagreed. "Isn't there something you'd like to ask?" he insisted. "This would seem to be a proper time for a question.

A pause in the middle of decisive action while there's still time to turn left or right." Matthew increased the range of the totoltetl's swings from hand to hand. Bruno lifted his head in response to the increased activity. "Admit it, Sarah," he insisted. "A question could be itching in your mind as well as mine. The same question."

"No," she said.

"Not about all this?" He was struck by the upheaval represented by the three piles of intimately familiar stuff. "I sure as hell have a question."

"Ask it," she said, nodding at the egg he was still tossing around.

"It's my question," he said defensively. "I'll just think it and roll the totoltetl."

"Fine. I didn't want to know actually."

"You're hiding from reality."

"No, I'm facing reality." She gestured at the room in upheaval.

"You've still got a problem about Iona," he said finally.

"No, I don't," she said. "Iona is dead. How can I have a problem with her?"

"That is one question that occurs to me."

"So go ahead and ask Mr. Totol."

Matthew nodded. He thought for a moment, then said, "Will Sarah ever forgive me for loving Iona?"

"I don't need to know your question." She shook her head and rolled her eyes toward the ceiling.

"Well, now you do, don't you," he said, positioning himself to roll the egg down a stretch of clear carpet. "Right is yes, left is no."

"It's presumptuous of that thing to know my mind."

"Do you have the answer, Sarah?"

"You're turning our life into a parlor trick."

"Here goes then."

After over two years of inactivity, the totoltetl moved down the carpet with an uncertain wobble; there seemed to be a timidity and a hesitation in its course. It rolled for about five feet directly toward

Bruno, who was following its course with a suspicious gaze. Then, the egg displayed a sudden decisiveness with a sharp 45-degree turn to the left. The dog let out an alarmed whoof as the egg came to a stop just inches away.

Matthew took a deep breath. "Well, that question has been answered."

"Yes," Sarah said.

He tightened his throat against the wave of grief that rose from his chest. "We haven't decided about Bruno, yet."

"Whatever you want," she said, "is fine with me."

"No Sarah, we'll settle this together. We adopted Bruno. He is our dog. We need to talk about Bruno."

"Fine," she nodded. "We'll ask Señor Totol one last question."

The dog let out a long mournful sound, somewhere between a moan and a yawn. Watchful of the egg in Mathew's hand, he stood on unsteady legs, ready to pounce, as if suddenly living up to his genetic coding as a hunter.

Mathew nodded at Sarah, their question unspoken in deference to Bruno's sensibilities; they had long assumed he knew when he was the subject of a discussion. "Go, Señor Totol," Mathew whispered. He smoothly sent the egg on its final roll.

The dog reared up and stared through bloodshot eyes at the path followed by the totoltetl. Its deep throaty bark seemed tinged with indignation, as if it understood and resented the influence the egg would have on its life. Bruno's destiny would not hinge on the roll of some fuzzy brown thing. It was in the dog's power to thwart the fates.

# Feast

Today, Thanksgiving, the house smells like sweat. Not the musky fragrance of recently exuded aerobic perspiration, but the dirty, bottom-of-the-clothes-basket kind. It's not the clean sweat that glistens on my father's brow when he's thinking hard or the pearly mustache beading above my mother's upper lip when she putters in her garden. Certainly not the sweet dancer's moisture that darkens Cousin Iris' leotard along her tight midriff and under her breasts when she's doing bar work. Today's smell is more like the sweat from my brother Ted's glands, a musty redolence incorporating Giorgio aftershave and hot tar from his road-repair job. The stink is finally traced to the kitchen where a 15lb turkey has been in the oven since dawn. I don't intend to eat any. This is a problem because food is a contentious thing for this family. If I keep up this attitude, I'll be sent packing again, for the fourth time.

That's a harsh possibility, considering that I was born to be here, among these fine people: a fate thing, I'm sure. I don't know that there was anything unusual about my birth; I haven't seen tapes or interviewed witnesses. Throughout the years I have undergone occasional rebirths via minivan. The exact circumstances of my comings and goings are muddled. Two years ago, I was supposed to be home for good; I continue to feel like a tourist.

Nobody ever asked my opinion regarding this household. It contains two official parents, one biological brother and one honorary cousin. But my inclinations toward vegetarianism, Marx, the goddess Kali, androgynous fashions, and cats are in conflict with the unambiguous preferences of the Ludemans.

On my latest trip home, I was handed a thick brown envelope with school transcripts, prescriptions, psychological evaluations, test scores (IQ 173, SATs 689 and 648, not bad for a slacker personality). An address was pinned to my T-shirt as if I were some kind of lobotomee who might get confused in the big city: The Ludemans, 328 Kimball Street, St. Paul, 651-798-3269.

My well-traveled suitcase with the scuffed corners and the taped handle was packed to bursting. The reason I crammed so many clothes into the suitcase is that I couldn't decide whether to pack male or female stuff. Sure, I know what I am; I've got eyes, there are mirrors. Genital considerations aside, from the age of eleven I could go either way, swinging to extremes: either soaking in bubbles under the morning light that flows like honey through the bathroom skylight, or rolling in the muddy backyard, a little boy-pig in pork heaven.

For the two-hour drive to St. Paul, I crammed a box of raisins for the sugar, sesame sticks for the salt, Diet Pepsi for energy. I had some books, including Das Kapital bound in black.

I started out as a slow reader, but when I finally got around to Marx, I knew he would be part of my intellectual baggage forever. The Big Karl has, through the years, given theoretical heft to my ideas, from "Communal Order in Wasps" (Show and Tell, Miss Hanteel's 6th grade Biology) to "The Irony of Martyrdom" (Term Paper, Mr. Steadman's 10th grade World History). People know better than to argue with me, when they realize my theories are backed up by KM. He's back in fashion in the better universities, too, now that he doesn't associate with Eastern European bureaucrats with cabbage breath.

When faced with even vaguely disagreeable situations, I'm content to lose myself in reading while letting the natural order of events take its course. Today, I get away from the kitchen smells by burying my nose in *Holes in the Air,* a novel about a young ghost and an old diva. I've been known to read a whole book without anyone seeing me blink. At one time, I used to pull out each page as I read it until the contents were scattered throughout the house, loose leaves slipped in behind furniture, under rugs and cushions, in the toilet. Some people hang on to books and find a permanent place for them, rows upon rows of them categorized by author, title, subject, color, size. I figured it takes courage to let a book go, to make room in your head for the next one.

I was releasing the story back into the ether. A good deed, I imagined.

Nowadays, my books with all their pages intact, end up wherever I happen to be when I finish them: the backseat of the car, their spines splayed from trying to hold them steady over the bumps and twists of the road, or water-swollen in a corner of the bathtub, or disappearing into the sand on some beach. They don't stay put for long; other pairs of eyes glom onto them. I was only a stop in their journey. Books, like me, are also tourists.

*\*\*\**

Ted, aka Brother Tedious, does not like books. Or the people who read them. He says that reading is like being dead to the world, life's experience reduced to black squiggles on white paper. That even television  is more active than that. I empathize with Tedious; he's a man of action. He's got feet the size of shoe boxes and hands like baseball mitts. For this meal he's in charge of mashing up the various tubers we're having. He takes the boiled sweet potatoes and presses them down with a special utensil that is basically a bunch of small holes with a handle. He takes a yam in his hand and shows it to me. When he holds it a certain way it looks like it has a nose, lips and chin.

"This is your head," he says. And then proceeds to squash it down into the bowl, its features now transformed into a dozen squishings wriggling out of the holes in the masher. He looks up at me and gives me his  devil grin.

Tedious is not yet a good-looking man. His face, in fact, is at the culminating point of his pimple-growing career; he may never again have as many pimples at one time as he does today. These zits are like living organisms with minds of their own. It's as if they had gathered, each one with its own consciousness, to colonize his head. As he smiles, an inflamed furuncle by the corner of his mouth gets squeezed into exuding a mixture of pus and blood. He scares the hell out of me with that grin of his.

I had planned on having sweet potatoes with little multi-colored marshmallows. Now it looks like I will just have the green beans with slivered almonds and fruit salad with the same little marshmallows as the yams. That, plus not-one-but-two kinds of pie should make for a balanced meal.

The next biggest person in the family is my father. His name is Al, aka Albert. He's a good guy, but hard to get to know. Years ago, before I arrived on the scene, he was fun-loving. He joked all the time. He was a ladies' man. He was voted most popular in his graduating class at Edison High School.

His mood changed one day when he complained that his head was growing. It wasn't so much a decision as a fear that came one time when he sat down at the dinner table, perhaps to a meal of turkey and gravy with giblets, like today's, and his head dropped down so low that his glasses got all fogged up by the steaming sections of flesh and gravy on his plate. He rolled his bewildered eyes up at my mother. "I don't know what happened," he said. "My head feels like a bowling ball."

"Excedrin might help," she offered.

Father's head became a persistent concern. For years he had worn a Greek sailor's cap, black with heavy embroidery on the bill. It occurred to him one day that the cap was tighter than he remembered it. After that, he was able to follow the gradual expansion, a millimeter at a time, of his head, until one day the headband had made a permanent crease along the sides of his skull.

Father has become a morose, reticent man who sits at the dinner table or in his favorite La-Z-Boy chair looking tired, his chin resting on the palm of his hand or his fist positioned under his jaw. My mother, who has a flair for words, put it best when she described her Al as a man who was forever carrying the weight of the world on his neck. It was around that time that Dad gave up reading, watching TV and going to movies. Now he makes it a point to avoid the news in any medium, from the daily paper to the radio traffic report, because he says, he can't really fit anything new inside his brain. He does watch old movies. He's gone through *Jailhouse Rock* and *The Fly* and *Gone With the Wind* many times. He also watches my cousin Iris.

I can understand that; we all ogle Iris. Which is okay, because she is not an actual biological relation. Iris was the daughter of Mother and Father's friends, the Fallons, who died when their airplane dropped out of the sky. She was six.

We like to look at Iris because her every movement is uncannily beautiful from start to finish. At sixteen, it's already clear she's a true dancer. The girl's simplest gesture is art, alive in the moment, a singular piece of deliberate grace never to be repeated again anywhere in the universe.

Even right now, it brings quiet tears to my eyes when I marvel at how precisely she holds her fork while making quick, delicate sawing movements with her knife on a piece of turkey. It's a brutal act performed with elegance. She then takes the morsel to her lips, her long slender hand seeming to float in midair, fingers poised like flower petals, her lips slightly parted. It's a moving thing.

\*\*\*

My mother's name is Camilla. She was a vastly more interesting person in the days before she met my father when she was a model and a poet. Sometimes she was both at the same time: art students sketched her nude while she recited verses to lift their minds from the carnal to the transcendent. She confessed to me once that she had at one time held great expectations of herself. But she came back to earth after she met Albert. There is clearly a pattern here, of the different members of my family stifling each other's potential.

"I was going to study with Gregory Gomez," she said. "I was fearless. I wanted to learn the sonnet, the sestina, the Homeric simile. Then, one day while I was sitting for a life drawing class, your father saw me through a window. He was selling the famous Mightyplate Roof Coating from Ft. Worth, Texas, and on his way to meet with the principal about the school's leaky roofs. He had his sample case with him, and he had decided to take a short cut through the school grounds. He stopped and looked up at me."

"Was it love at first sight?"

"At the time I thought it was simple voyeurism. There I was without a care in the world, holding my skinny body in a natural-looking contortion, when I saw this man outside with his pear-shaped head and wide amazed eyes. I suddenly froze. My heart was beating like crazy, and I was gasping for air. I couldn't move at all; I stood on the platform and reached for my clothes.

"It took a while before people realized what was happening. I mean, the kids were staring up at me, studying my every pore and bump, and Albert was looking puzzled as it started to dawn on him that he may have had something to do with my sudden discomfiture. All he could think of doing was smile at me kindly, and wait for me to get dressed, while the students held their pencils poised and complained about being left hanging from a breast or stranded in a buttock.

"In the end, I scurried out the door. Albert caught up with me and apologized about a dozen times. Then he pleaded to see me home."

\*\*\*

Camilla opens the oven door and turkey effluvium invades every corner of the house. She leans in with a giant dropper and sucks up turkey sweat from the bottom of the pan and squirts it all along its back and sides. The bird is naked and scrunched up, appearing vulnerable and ashamed. Kind of the way this whole family seems to feel about nudity.

In fact, the only one among us who walks around naked is Iris. And that only in the middle of the night, when she steps out nude from her bed and saunters down the hall to pee.

I may be the only one that's been lucky enough to have seen her. One time we nearly bumped into each by the bathroom. I had on my pajamas and she was a vision of moonlit skin. I whispered "Well, hello, Iris," as we crossed, acting as if the sight of her hadn't taken my breath away.

"You should try sleeping in the nude," she murmured, in her world-class dancer voice. "It makes the night tres sensual."

That night I put away my pajamas, and haven't worn them since. I have also sauntered down the hall in the middle of the night but have never again crossed paths with Iris. I have however stumbled into Tedious who said I looked like a turnip, and my father who told me it was unsanitary to sleep in the nude, and my mother who warned that if the house caught fire I would not be properly dressed for the escape.

Now, as we all sit around the table, I delight in the secret thought that Iris and I have something meaningful in common. It means our skin shares a nightly experience of silky-smooth sheets, each individual fiber seeming to find a pore to tickle and rub. It means that when we dream, we dream with our entire bodies. But most important it means that we are open to new experiences, courageous enough to be ready for whatever the fates may send us in the night. I've never found a chance to tell her this.

On special occasions our family likes to dress up. Tedious puts on a white shirt and a tie. Albert actually removes his cap and slicks his hair back with a dab of old-fashioned brilliantine which he gets from Argentina, and which leaves his hair glossy black, as slick and shiny as patent leather. Iris wears a black dress that makes her white skin look luminescent. Mother wears pearls. And I wear one of my mother's old church dresses.

I like the style, with the full skirt and the blousy sleeves and the neat row of brass buttons along the front. The overall effect is capped by a leopard skin pillbox hat I shop-lifted at a vintage store. The look is cute in a beefy kind of way, the refined lady gone aerobolic.

*** 

"White or dark?" Father asks holding the carving fork in his right hand. He looks at me straight in the eye but doesn't let on that he thinks my attire is in any way strange.

"Neither." I smile throughout this whole exchange. "I have a contract with turkeys," I say. "We have agreed not to eat each other."

"You're going to die if you don't eat," he says, pointing the carving knife at me.

It sounds like a threat. There are places around the world where people would kill for a slice of turkey. Here, it's the opposite; reality stands on its ear. I love contradictory logic.

"Okay, I love life," I say. "A bit of white meat, please."

He glances at the knife, which he holds in a menacing position. Then laughs, as if it had just explained the joke to him. "I meant that you need the protein." Still chuckling, he looks to his right and his left, and mother smiles along with him, and Tedious shakes his head with exaggerated incredulity. Even Iris rolls her eyes and sticks out her tongue at me. What a traitor. I love her anyway; it's her tongue that makes the moment.

I hold out my plate graciously because I know how much trouble and expense the family has gone to for this meal. Still, even if he didn't mean he would personally kill me for not eating turkey, the thought had wormed its way into my subconscious.

By now my plate is piled high with slices of turkey drowned in gravy with bits of the bird's most private organs floating about. Tedious has piled my plate high with his potatoes and yams and Iris has served me a huge helping of green beans with slivered almonds. The plate weighs a ton. I look around the table and decide that I have more food in front of me than the four of them put together. Mountains of it sit there steaming before me, sending up sweaty vapors.

Suddenly, out comes a camera and the flash goes *Pop! Pop!* in front of my eyes. I get it: It's a joke. A family joke. I don't let on that anything is even slightly strange. I don't ask them what the hell they think is so interesting about me today that they need to record it for posterity. Is it the clothes I'm wearing? They've seen them before. That this may be the last time in my life that I will ingest turkey? Big deal. The frightened look in my eyes as I eat for my life? Yes, and how cruel. The old Eat-to-Live adage in living color. I straighten out the leopard-skin pillbox hat, which is about to teeter off my head, and proceed to dig in.

Ah, how I dig. In contrast to Iris' delicate ballet of the knife and fork, I am spearing large chunks of breast and then driving the meat into the hills and mounds of yam and beans, flying finally into my wide-open mouth. *Pop!* goes the flash. Ha, this is fun. Even as I'm attempting to masticate this clump down to size, I'm already plunging the fork into a dive for the next bite.

It occurs to me that I've lived this moment before. That I'm only repeating a ritual that can't be exhausted, that time after time, it must be relived with undiminished intensity. A fork dives and soars like an airplane doing acrobatics. The engines roar and whine as the payload is lifted up into the sky and brought down with ballistic precision into the open cavern of my mouth. Watch it, here it goes! *Hmmm, chew chew, yummie, swallow.*

After a couple of passes I look around the table. Nobody is laughing anymore; they're doing their best not to look at me. I glance from Tedious who is staring blankly at some point in space above my head, to Iris who is concentrating on picking the almonds out of the green beans, to Albert who is staring at my mother at the other end of the table in a silent appeal for help. I also turn to flash her a grin.

Mother seems about to cry. Carefully she leans toward me with a spoon and gathers the remnants of turkey gravy that have stayed on my chin. She spoons these out and then hands me a napkin. I put the napkin down on the table and spear about thirty green beans on my fork.

"Every year, it's the same disgusting thing," Tedious mutters under his breath.

He has no right to say this. He has bits of pink and white marshmallow clinging to his mustache. He is wrong of course, it's not the same thing every year, but as I open my mouth to explain the only thing that comes out is a series of muffled grunts.

"I've lost my appetite," Ted pushes back his chair and crumples his napkin on the table.

"For Christ's sake," Father says. "Can't we all be together as a family one day a year?" He looks at Mother as if his question hadn't been totally rhetorical.

"Of course," she might say, "We're together as a family, a wonderfully extended family if you take Iris into account, and we're together every moment of our lives, whether we are sitting at the table or not."

But this is not what Mother says. What she does say is, "I'm so sorry."

"Sorry for what?" I ask angrily, but nobody understands what I've said because my mouth is still full. "I mean, you wanted me to eat, right?" My mouth goes hlumph, hlumph.

Albert gets up from the table and takes his plate to the La-Z-Boy in front of the TV. He settles down to watch a replay of the famous 1976 Super Bowl.

"Eat up before it gets cold," Mother says to the only ones left at the table, namely Iris and me.

"It's still pretty warm." I press my palm onto the heaping platter, as if to check its temperature, and let the warm ooze of stuffing and potatoes and gravy-soaked turkey seep between my fingers. It feels nice. It feels better than it tastes. I have visions of the different flavors and textures getting into my body through the pores in the skin, finding their way into the capillary network, entering the bloodstream, swimming around the system putting a little sweetness here, a little savory there, making the blood redder and richer. I bypass the middle organs and get right to the heart of the matter.

I look up at Iris and think that she can really understand this tactile stuff, the old touchy-feely as they say, a naked kind of thing with nothing in the way between the brain and the food. Talk about sensuous. No, don't talk about it; do it. "Hey Iris. Put your hand on it. It's like eating naked."

"I thought that was our secret," she says. And for a moment there, I think she's going to give me that sly grin of hers. But no, her lips are pressed tight, her eyes are squinting mean thoughts at me. She puts down her knife and fork, lining them up alongside each other on the edge of the plate. Then she stands up, smooths down the back of her pretty dress and says, "Excuse me," to my mother. "I need to make a call." She says nothing to me.

It's just Mother and me now. Like in the old days. And like other rough times, it looks as if we're going to have a talk. She takes her chair and pulls it around the table to sit beside me. Then she takes a napkin, dips it in water and lifts my hand off the plate and wipes it clean. I start to put my other hand down on the now not-so- warm mass of holiday victuals, when she takes it by the wrist and bends it back until I cry out. She then pushes the plate so it's beyond my reach.

"I think I should go back," I say.

"Are you happier there than at home?"

"They eat what I do."

"*All* the attendants are vegetarian?" She's not taking me seriously.

"They range from vegan to fishoterian. I fit right in."

"After all these years." She starts to weep. "Back and forth, back and forth."

"Not always my idea."

"We should have never sent you away in the first place," she sniffs.

"Terrible things could've happened, Mom," I give her a little jab on the shoulder. "I have considered castrating Tedious, seducing Iris."

I don't qualify for the Clean Plate Club this year. An hour from the time I sat down at the table, the mountain of sliced flesh and mashed tubers sits lumpily before me under a translucent sheath of congealing gravy. Mother gave up trying to have a conversation with me, and left, barely stifling a sob. Brother Tedious, in charge of cleaning up, picked up around me, loading up on silverware, the big platter with the dismembered bird, the sloshing gravy boat, four plates licked clean. I remain alone, knowing that I won't eat any more, but afraid to cross the living room where I know I will have to face my destiny, again.

Finally, unwilling to consider the lifeless remnants of my friend the turkey any longer, I rise from the table and edge out of the dining room, hugging the wall along the stairs to my room. I keep my head from looking toward the living room, even though out of the corner of my eye I can see Albert, Ted, Iris and Mother all sitting next to each other on the blue couch. They look primed for confrontation.

"Come here," Albert says softly. "We need to have a talk."

Well, it just about cracks me up to hear him call me over, so tenderly, so sadly, knowing that I have let him down in the worse way.

"Now?" I ask hoping he will say, *No not now, not this minute, a little later maybe*.

"Yes, now," he says. "But it can wait while you change out of that getup."

"I'll be right back." I gather the skirt hem in one fist and, hanging on to the banister for balance with the other hand, clamber up the stairs two steps at a time.

I go straight into my parents' bedroom and start rummaging through their closet. I pull out, hastily, a pair of Albert's plaid golf pants (very St. Paul, Minnesota ca. 1983), a gray silk shirt with french cuffs, a double-breasted blazer with a nautical insignia.

"Who the hell do you think you are?" Albert says when I enter the living room to face the tribunal.

"I am my father's son," I answer. "And my mother's daughter," I add, meeting my mom's tear-filled eyes. "My brother's sibling and my cousin's cousin. I am part of this family."

*** 

The blue suitcase waits by the front door. Either Ted or Albert must've brought it down. I *clop clop* to it in my clown shoes, squat unsteadily and unsnap the latches. Everything is there. Das Kapital, my collected papers through the tenth grade, a six pack of Diet Pepsi, my pills. The only clothes in it are my pajamas. "Thanks for a thoughtful gesture!" I shout, in case Iris is around to appreciate the irony.

I close it up quickly. No goodbye, no look back, no second thoughts. I step out into the chilly evening and sit down on the doorstep to wait for my ride. I say to myself that whatever comes first, ambulance, taxi, van, I'll ride it. I search in the pockets of my father's blue blazer for the sealed envelope containing the two-page letter from my family, which I'm supposed to hand to the attendants. I could read it, if I wanted to.

# Carlos and Artemisa

## I - The Beautiful Wife

In the time that it took to raise a glass of real champagne, acquired at a good price from a friend in the Mexican Consulate in San Diego, make a silent toast to her fifty-second wedding anniversary, and quaff the whole thing, Doña Artemisa Valle decided that her husband had to go.

She had no idea where Don Carlos should be. Another building, another city, another country. The farther the better: Alaska. What could be farther and bleaker and more isolated for a Mexican than Alaska. She pictured him in an igloo, his pudgy body wrapped in bear fur, a three-day beard sprouting in his cheeks, his stiff frostbitten fingers clutching the leather-bound notebook where he had been writing his memoirs every afternoon since moving from Mexico City to Santa Alma, California twenty years ago.

She looked around the table at her daughter Carmen, at her son Luis, at her husband, and was grateful that none of them could read minds. She held her glass out for her son to refill, and this time took small, delicate sips. The bubbles tickled her nose and she burst out laughing. She was seventy years old and, contrary to expectations, she was enjoying life. If her husband chose to mope around, then he should do it someplace where his moods wouldn't affect innocent bystanders.

45

Artemisa watched her husband pick at the cake, fastidiously separating the layers so that he could scrape away more of the cream filling with the edge of his fork. "But what are you doing, viejo?" she exclaimed. "You think a pound or two on that old carcass matters to me? Enjoy yourself, amor. It's our anniversary."

"It's too sweet," he grimaced.

"Too sweet," she mimicked. "Too salty, too oily, too big, too this, too that. You have to enjoy life."

"I'm too busy surviving," he said, "without the extra requirement of having to enjoy the process as well."

\*\*\*

Everybody agreed that, upon her return the night before from her latest trip to Dr. Illhoffer's famous Living Cells Clinic in Elloesberg, Switzerland, Artemisa looked younger and more beautiful. Even with the flight to San Diego arriving hours late, and then the sleepy drive through the hills to Santa Alma, there was a special glow to her skin, still smooth and nutty brown and luminous, the sparkle in her black eyes twinkling wherever she gazed.

Waiting at the airport to give her big abrazos was Carmen, who had obtained leave from her convent in Los Angeles. Beside her stood Luisito, who was her favorite because he had deep dark eyes just like hers. Missing was the youngest daughter, Marcela, who had broken her promise to lead a moral life and therefore was banned from family occasions.

Seeing her children at the airport had cheered Artemisa because she had felt very alone on the long flight back from Zurich. What kind of company is a husband who laments constantly, and who already smells like an old man because his inner gases are seeping out of every pore in his body?

Naturally, she had felt glad to be alone in her own separate room for the fourteen days' stay at Dr. Illhoffer's clinic, because Carlos was apt to ruin the good effects of the $7,500 injections of cells drawn from the vital organs of a freshly aborted lamb fetus, with his malingering and negativity, and especially his sudden bursts of concupiscence, too odd in a man his age to be charming. Wouldn't you know, on the eve of receiving the first dose of the Living Cells, when they were both supposed to be resting their bodies and calming their minds with a fruit fast and meditation, the silly old man attained a sturdy erection, his first in months, and in the middle of the night slinked down the hallway to her room. Of course, she couldn't deny him his pleasure; a wife has her duties. She managed nevertheless to keep a restful mind. Yet she was sure that the life of the lamb sacrificed for his benefit had been totally wasted on her husband.

She was explaining all this to her daughter, Hermana María del Carmen in the convent, dressed in a high-buttoned blouse and a gray skirt whose hem grazed the tops of her boxy lace-up shoes. Then, turning to her Luis, all in black leather that still smelled pungently new, she hooked her arm in his and looked up at him with her flirtatious eyes.

Luis had hired the limousine for the ride to Santa Alma. When Artemisa saw the cream-colored stretch driven by a handsome Anglo in blue military cap and a crisp white shirt, she insisted they take photos.

"After all, I've been gone for two weeks, and I am a changed woman. Sí, Luisito, we'll take pictures so we can remember when we're no longer beautiful."

She unbuttoned her dark green silk coat to reveal a salmon blouse and a black leather skirt cut well above the knee. She held a square cosmetics bag that matched the rest of her six-piece red luggage set which the driver had lined up in front of the limo. She froze her hand in midair in the middle of blowing a kiss and waited for the click. "Stand up straight," she coaxed Carlos. "Otherwise, people will realize that you are getting shorter and shorter with every passing year. I didn't marry a chaparro."

"Vieja," he said patiently. "We are both shrinking. It's the passing years. They get heavy."

"Speak for yourself," Artemisa said, pulling herself erect, placing her fists on her waist, and tilting her head back defiantly. "Shoot the picture, *hijito*," she said. "I want to share this, the most vital night of my life, with my friends on the Facebook."

\*\*\*

In the mornings, Artemisa rises early, often while it's still dark out. She has her coffee, thick and sweet and fragrant of cinnamon, just like in Mexico, on the terrace of her eighteenth-floor condominium right on the coast. While her husband sleeps, she enjoys the gradual unfolding of the fog the hides the ocean, the rising sun burning away the layers of mist to reveal the rocky shore, the secluded beaches, the rows of tall palms along the coastal highway that meanders north to Del Mar and San Juan Capistrano and Los Angeles.

The highway also leads south to Tijuana. But Artemisa does not like to think of the country they left twelve years before, traveling at night like gangsters in a black car loaded down with money—dollars, not pesos—the three kids squabbling in the back seat, their parents up front, praying that the results of the surprise audit of the Procurement Office that Carlos ran would not be made public while they were still in Mexico. Not that Artemisa felt they had anything to be ashamed of. There were unwritten rules for government work, chief of which were that for six years you worked fourteen hours a day, seven days a week; you ruined your health with ritual drinking and endless gorging; and you watched your back for disgruntled leftists and greedy underlings. In exchange, you made your money. The fact that Carlos Valle had been singled out for an investigation was unfortunate timing, the result of a suddenly bankrupt economy, which got fingers pointing in every direction. Now, they felt comfortable among friends in a high-rise where so many Mexicans lived that the compound had been nicknamed Taco Towers by jealous Anglos. Their nest-egg was locked away in a Grand Cayman trust. She was proud of her husband for making all this happen.

Doña Artemisa was not one to brood; she had calls to make this morning. "Querida," she greeted her friend Sarita Bustamante, whose brother's construction firm had built most of the airports in Mexico. "You won't believe how wonderful the food was, and yet I lost five kilos. They serve you tiny, tiny portions. And everything is so fresh! You can actually see them churning the butter in the little Swiss village for your lunch later in the day. How do I feel, you ask? I am so deliciously skinny you have to see to believe. It's a miracle. Carlitos? He is exactamente the same as always."

"Querida," she said to her friend Marta Galdós, who was the widow of a former head of Pemex, the oil company. "I am wonderful. But very worried about Carlitos. He is becoming a depressive. Some days I just don't think I can manage him. All he did in Switzerland was complain of being left alone in his room, about the food, the doctors, the language. Can you believe it? He actually told Dr. Illhoffer that they were a gang of charlatans, that if not for me he wouldn't be taking the Living Cells, and that he was watching me in case I decided to squander all our money on their voodoo treatments. Yes, I've been married to him for fifty-two years, but between his outbursts and his moping I'm at a loss."

"Querida!" she exclaimed to her friend Doris Macias who had been the special friend of the governor of Guanajuato way back when the exchange rate was twelve pesos and fifty centavitos for one dollar. "I am going to have to do something with this man. Carlitos is making me crazy. He does nothing all day but watch TV and fret about our money. Of course, we have enough to get by, in a nice way, you understand. He is worried that the government is going to take it away from him. No, not the US, the Mexicans. Imagine."

Carlos Valle awoke to the sound of his wife's voice. The happy, energetic cadence of her chatter, was a sign that his wife had been up for hours. His reward for the long night of wide-awake insomnia was this time of sweet slumber after his wife was up.

That morning he felt relieved that he no longer had to push his way against the crowds in the Zurich airport, then squeeze himself into the narrow seat of the crowded 747, where they rode coach at his insistence so they would not attract attention by sitting up front, and finally arguing about the validity of their immigration documents with a surly INS official who treated them like wetbacks.

The worst moment of the trip had happened in the small men's shop in Geneva where Artemisa had taken him, insisting that a man of his position shouldn't go around with frayed cuffs and collars that curled up at the tips. Pinpoint ceiling lights cast a warm glow over the brass-edged mahogany counter on which a prim man with manicured nails displayed, as if they were jewels, a selection of silk ties, lizard-skin belts, and Sea Island cotton shirts. From across the store, Carlos became aware of a short, squat man with brown skin and black hair and a rippled neck who had been leafing through a book of fabric swatches but was now staring in his direction.

"Buenos días," he said when his eyes met Carlos's. With a small bow toward Artemisa, he added, "It is interesting how one can hear voices from Mexico anywhere in the world these days."

Carlos turned to nod politely at the man, before he was drawn by Artemisa into inspecting another stack of shirts which the clerk had placed on the counter. "It is a small world," Carlos said with a shrug.

"And getting smaller every day," the man continued affably. "Which part of Mexico are you from?"

"We are from San Diego, California," Artemisa said coolly.

"Ah, yes, I understand perfectly," the man said. "But before that, you lived in Mexico, no?"

"Mexico City," Carlos nodded. "But we have been in the United States many, many years."

"Since before la crisis?" The man smiled broadly, displaying two gold-capped incisors on either side of his mouth. "Or after."

"I think you should try the button-down collar for a change," Artemisa said to her husband, putting her fingers over his wrist and pulling him away from the stranger. "It would give you a more youthful look."

"The señor certainly looks young," the stranger said. "Is this a good place to buy shirts?" he asked. "Would you say this is the best city in Europe for men's attire? You seem to be very knowledgeable, señora," he smiled at Artemisa. "I myself just came in here today for the first time. But the prices are high, if you think in terms of pesos."

"One pays for quality," Artemisa said.

"Easier if you have dollars, or better, francs," the man said, pushing away the swatch book. "I think I will look into other stores before I decide." Then, as he was about to go out the door, he turned again and said apologetically, "Forgive me, I have been rude. My name is Miguel Guerrero." He stepped up to Carlos offering his hand.

"S-S-Suárez." Carlos felt a warm glow on his face. "José Suárez, and my wife Ana María."

"*Muchísimo gusto*," the man said effusively. "I thought you looked familiar for a second," he added. "In any case, it is always nice to encounter compatriots, no?"

***

Now, emerging from his dark bedroom into the brilliant morning light that came through the window facing the ocean, Carlos could not shake the feeling of dread that the man in the shop had recognized him. The squat dark figure in the metallic brown polyester suit and the no-longer fashionable flowered tie could have been any one of a dozen men who had worked for the Ministry of Public Works back in the years when Carlos Valle was heading the Procurement Office.

"He looked as he was about to insult me," Carlos said to Artemisa, catching her off guard as if he deliberately meant to confuse her with his comments that seemed to come out of thin air.

"Who, mi amor? Who would want to insult the sweetest man in the world?"

"The man in Geneva," he said testily, impatient at the thought that she was playing games when she surely knew who he was talking about. "The Mexican who was making believe he was buying shirts."

51

"All in your imagination," Artemisa sniffed. "He is just another bureaucrat with more pretensions than cash."

"I was nervous," Carlos murmured.

"You thought quickly and gave him a false name. We are not under any obligation to socialize with people just because they happen to be from Mexico."

"I'm scared even now, years after," Carlos admitted. "The government has people looking into the affairs of some of us who left."

"Tonto," Artemisa laughed. "Look out the window." She pulled Carlos to the edge of the terrace. Below, the ocean glimmered in the sun, spotted with huge splashes of a blue deeper than the color of the whole, then fragmenting against the rocks in brilliant crystalline explosions. "See that? You can look out your window and say to yourself that you own that ocean, and nobody will come up here to contradict you."

"It makes me queasy to look down," Carlos said, stepping back from the terrace railing.

\*\*\*

In the afternoon, Carlos Valle worked on his Memorias. He read from the first page of the notebook:

> I was born in 1927. Nobody could have guessed at the time the evil I would later be capable of doing. From my first childhood memories, I felt destined for great things, to be a humanitarian, a scientist, a man of letters. But when I moved to Santa Alma, still young at sixty, I had accomplished everything I was meant to in life: I was married to Artemisa; I was the father of Luis, Carmen and Marcela; I had seven suitcases packed with one-hundred dollar bills, dozens of cashiers checks made out in different amounts to different banks, and hundreds of gold coins wrapped in newspaper so they

wouldn't rub against each other. Only Artemisa knows for sure how much it all came to. We left in the middle of the night, Artemisa and I taking turns driving a big Range Rover, the kids in the back seat, the money in the trunk. The only thing I missed from Mexico was my dog Azabache, a tall Labrador with a lustrous black coat. We left the dog behind, with a bowl of water. The house with all the furniture and clothes in the closets and food in the refrigerator I signed over to my friend in the Ministry of Foreign Relations, who issued diplomatic passports for the whole family. My friend, from what I hear, is still living in my big, beautiful house in Coyoacán. I hope he takes good care of Azabache.

Even as Carlos turned to the next page, he knew it would remain blank. In the several months since he had begun, he had been unable to write further. The simple beginning seemed to so conclusively wrap up the story of his life that there wasn't anything left for him to add. To fill the remaining three hundred pages with prevarication, excuses, and finally, apologies, seemed a waste of time. But still he sat every afternoon at his writing table, and for an hour or two, he waited. It was not that he didn't remember. He could at any time close his eyes and see the details of his life in the Office of Procurement. The lengthy contracts for streetlights or park benches or public restrooms, though he knew the villages would remain dark, that there were no parks in which to put the benches, that the poor would continue to shit in vacant lots. There were the daily brown envelopes, crammed so full that the seams had to be bound in tape to keep them from splitting and exuding wrinkled, oily currency all over his desk. The lengthy quality inspection reports for bridges and dams and roads that had been contracted and actually designed but never built. Many even had names, such as the Benito Juarez Dam or the Hidalgo Highway, and they were all put in files along with the fictional evidence of their shadowy existence:

phony contracts, competitive bids, purchase orders, payroll lists, quality certification. The system had existed for decades.

The problem did not lie with Carlos's memory then, but with the need that the Memorias be true, a record of the death of his soul, a confession to be made public only after his death. He could picture his children discovering the notebook tucked unobtrusively next to his cherished *Chronicles of Bernal Díaz*, the poetry of Sor Juana, the translations of ancient Nahuatl texts, and in this fine company, *Las Memorias de Don Carlos Valle*. His son Luis would not understand his shame. Carmen would refuse to read them. Only Marcela would realize that what he needed was forgiveness.

Marcela was the bright one, but Artemisa had banished her from the family for breaking the promise she had made as a fourteen-year-old, that she would remain a virgin until her wedding day. Artemisa had extracted the vow from the girls as they were leaving Mexico. Unless Carmen and Marcela swore sexual abstinence, she would turn the car around and drive them back to the house in Coyoacán where they would be safe from poaching gringo men.

Once a year, Artemisa and the girls went to see Dr. Alonso, a gynecologist with an office just south of the border in Tijuana. He specialized in hormone therapies not available on the US. side. As a special service to the Valle family, he would examine Marcela and Carmen, and confirm their virginity.

The certification had gone on normally, Carlos learned later from Marcela, until two years ago when she was twenty-two and seeing a boyfriend, not an Anglo, but a fine Mexican fellow she had met in one of her classes at the law school. Dr. Alonso took a look at the reflection in his speculum and then, without a word to Marcela, marched out to reveal the latest development to Artemisa, who was after all, the client that paid his substantial fee.

Artemisa gave Marcela one week to leave the house, but that same night the young woman moved right into the apartment of her friend, Gustavo Eloy. Carlos had tried to prevail upon his wife not to send the girl away, but Artemisa insisted that she was the one responsible for the children's morals and it was her duty to act accordingly. He loved Marcela more than his other children mainly because he understood her best. Carmen with her intoxication with Jesus and the Guadalupe and the saints constantly churning in her heart, seemed exotic and a little disturbed. Luisito, who at thirty-five was the eldest, was content to sleep all day and then spend his nights in bars where everyone showed off their leather outfits. Carlos sensed that there was more to his son's mysterious ways than an interest in motorcycles. But Artemisa was resolutely clueless.

He closed the notebook and leaned back from the massive oak table that reminded him of the study he had as a lawyer in private practice. The colors had been rich and warm, mostly brown and leather and polished brass, and the desk large enough for him to spread upon it the massive notary books that contained in fine spidery penmanship the details of wills and testaments, transfers of property, corporations' by-laws. The big leather chair creaked as he reached for the phone. He smiled in anticipation of the pleasure he derived from chatting with his daughter.

"Marcelita."

"You're back, Papito," she said cheerfully. "Are you younger?"

Carlos chuckled at her good-natured skepticism. "Those things work better on your mother. She gets revitalized. I end up with little more than a sore butt."

"That's because you have no faith."

He pictured her smiling at him. "I had ten thousand dollars' worth of faith."

"I take it back," she laughed. "*Es mucha tu fé.*"

"How are you, Marcela?" he asked seriously. "Are you happy still?"

"Sí, Papá. Very happy."

"Good. You are the happiest in the family. Your sister has a very grim marriage to Jesus. Your brother is still sleeping. And your mother is happy only when she's talking or shopping."

"And you, Papi, how are you doing?"

"I've been better, Marcelita."

"You need to get out of the house."

"That's also what your mother says."

"I'll come by for you tomorrow, and we'll have lunch by the beach."

"No, perhaps not the beach," he said. "It is too wide open. It gives me a lost feeling."

"Then our apartment."

"That would be better. You can send for pizza."

"You remember," she laughed. "It's the specialty of the house."

*** 

Artemisa lay awake most of the night. There was no way a woman could sleep in peace when down the hall she knew her husband was rattling his old bones around, turning this way and that inside his little dark room, his shrunken body swamped by the big silk pajamas.

They had been married so long that, even if they didn't speak about it, she knew what he was thinking during his endless nights. He was thinking that he was nothing more than a toad, hovering about in a shallow corner of some dark swamp, that he was no better than a fly settling its furry little legs down on a mound of cow dung, that he was a worm burrowing deep into the loamy black earth of the fallow winter fields. All because of the six years he spent in government. All because of her. Because she had not been happy with the small pickings of his legal practice; she had looked around at the other women in their circle and wept at the thought of all the fine things they could buy abroad and which she couldn't even afford to go look at.

Throughout the years they had both been aware of a solemn contract, certainly unwritten, even unspoken, yet binding from the day of their wedding: she would be the most beautiful wife the little man could possibly aspire to, and he would become wealthy for her.

Neither had counted on the bookish lawyer having the intellect to solve problems and the skills to manage a huge bureaucracy, but not the character to plunder. Some men had an ear for music, or a heart for poetry, or hands for surgery. But Carlos Valle had no stomach for larceny. When he began his tenure in the Procurement Office and his secret bank accounts started to bulge as if dam gates had been opened, his first thought was that something was wrong with his bowels, perhaps an ulcer or colitis, pray to God nothing more serious. Through those six years, poor Don Carlitos could keep nothing down but boiled potatoes, jars of Gerber's baby food, and warm glasses of frothing milk to ease the acid that crawled like serpents' tongues up to the back of his throat.

She knew it was to her husband's credit that in spite of his lack of natural ability, he kept opening his arms to the flood of suppliers' gifts, the kickbacks from contractors, the bribes from the army of quality inspectors that descended in his name to check every kilometer of highway, every foot of bridge work, every brick of warehouse construction that came under his domain. She could not forget that her gentle husband had given up his health for her.

For the third time that night, she heard him carefully open the door to his bedroom and rush on bare feet to the bathroom down the hall. She marveled how one small person could piss so many times. She herself would never wake up at odd hours it weren't for her husband's insomnia which was as contagious as the flu.

"Are you all right, mi vida?" she called out from her bed.

"Yes, go back to sleep," he said peering into the dark. "I didn't mean to wake you, querida."

"You know I can't sleep if you are having troubles."

"Not troubles," he insisted. "Just thoughts."

After a moment, seeing that he remained at her door, holding it open just enough to let in a sliver of light from the hallway, she added, "Are you going to stand there all night? Come to my bed for a little while, *viejito*."

He lay on his back beside her, very still, their bodies not quite touching but close enough for him to feel the warmth of her flesh, the scent from her skin, the slight rise and fall of the blanket with her breathing.

"Why can't you be happy, Carlitos?" she murmured.

He shrugged off her question. "Are you happy, Artemisa?"

"At our age, if we are not happy with the life we've made, we might as well die."

"I suppose we ought to be satisfied," he ventured.

"Listen to me, viejo," she said, sitting up on the bed. "It's a dog's life any way you look at it. When you're rich you dance like a dog, all happy and excited, tongue hanging out, tail wagging. When you're poor, you eat like a dog. "

"I'm having lunch with Marcelita tomorrow," he chuckled. "She's calling for pizza."

"She's poor because she wants to be."

"And we're rich because we want to be rich?"

"No, Carlos. Because God wants us to be. You've never understood that?"

"She's happy."

"Go back to your own bed." She gave his back a shove with her small fist. "I am happy too. If you can't be happy with me, then maybe you should go live with your daughter."

"Don't take it like that. It was just a comment."

"Buenas noches, Carlitos," she said, and gathered the covers close around her.

He nodded, even though she was no longer looking at him because she had turned away to face the wall. She heard him leave the room, closing the door very softly behind him. In the morning she would call Marcela and forgive her. Then she would make a proposition to her: "Your father misses you." She would send her a check to help her rent a larger apartment.

## II: In the Exile Zone

Artemisa Valle knocks on the door to the men's room off the lobby of the Del Marqués Hotel. She listens for a response, raps louder, more insistently. "I seem to have lost my husband," she mutters to a couple that stops to stare at her. The wife does the Anglo rolling-of-the-eyes. Artemisa opens the door a crack and speaks loudly for the benefit of the woman. "Carlos, *querido. Estás bien?*"

Usually, Artemisa delights in being noticed. Confident of not looking a day over fifty-nine, her very black hair is pulled back into a glossy chignon; a leather skirt shows off her legs; a bright red halter top under the short black leather jacket offers a glimpse of pancaked breasts. She knows that at seventy, death can come unexpectedly, but she will go in a blaze rather than sink into the nunnish weeds of her mother's generation back in Mexico.

She waits for the couple to move on, and tentatively slips inside. "Hola," she calls out, her voice echoing against the black and white tiled walls. "Anybody there?"

Leave it to her husband to disappear in the middle of a leisurely lunch with their friends Betty and Pedro Macías, at the best table in the finest restaurant with the most spectacular ocean view in all of San Diego. Carlos considered Pedro a pompous windbag. But he adored Betty.

"You're jealous," Artemisa teased him.

"Of what? Pedro has to take a pill to get his *pito* up."

"No, *querido*, not jealous because of Betty. Of his money."

"He stole more than anyone. I would rather sleep at night."

"None of us sleeps well, Carlitos. The less money we have, the worse we sleep."

Now, this perfectly enjoyable luncheon has been disrupted by Carlos' disappearance. She imagines him losing his way through the crowded lobby to stop and chat; he's always running into familiar faces from his days in government. It's up to her to pull him back.

"Artemisa," her husband rasps from within the men's room.

"*Querido!*" she says, stepping boldly inside. She can't help looking at the row of gleaming porcelain urinals, their bowls cupped in anticipation, chrome handles within easy reach. They remind her of Las Vegas slot machines, though less festive in their whiteness.

Carlos lies prone on the floor, facing the wall, his arms bent toward the shoulders as if he had been doing push-ups. She rushes to him, her heels unsteady on the marble floor. "*Viejo,*" she says. "What on earth has happened to you?"

"I fell," he says.

She kneels down to examine his face. He seems fine except for the disarray in his wispy gray hair. "You just fell? No one just falls."

"I did," he snaps. "As you can see."

She notices the pale outline of the missing watch on his wrist. "Can you get up?"

"I'm not sure," he says.

"I'll help you." She starts to pull him up by one arm when he shocks her with a sudden cry. He continues to whimper even after she lets go.

Two young fellows come into the men's room. Artemisa is aware of the curious Pietá-like tableau she and Carlos make but suspects the pathos of the composition is lost on the boys.

"Wow, lady, you're in the..."

"Call 911," Artemisa says. "And zip up your pants."

"What?" They are slow to understand the situation.

"Telephone. Emergency. 9-1-1. Am I not speaking English?"

"I'll call," the brighter one says rushing out the door.

The other one steps up to a urinal. "I don't mean to be disrespectful, ma'am," he slurs. "But this needs to happen right now."

She grants her permission with a wave of her fingers.

"I think I've broken something," Carlos mutters.

"Don't be so negative, *querido.*"

\*\*\*

The X-rays show a ghostly landscape traversed by white winding streams representing jagged fissures in both shoulders. On this, his first night at home after a restless stay at the hospital, Don Carlos Valle seems unaware of Sarah Jardine, the nurse standing next to his wife. Shrinking inside his silk robe, wildly red with black spidery embroidery, he slouches into a wingback chair in the sitting room by his bedroom. A few inches of white hairless ankle are visible between the tops of droopy blue socks and his pajamas. His arms, cradled by slings made of brown elasticized fabric, are rigidly crossed at his midriff. In the curtained gloom, his head tilted to one side, one soft hand resting over the remote control on his lap, Carlos slumps through the drone of a talk show on Univision. He feigns sleep.

Artemisa steps to the window and parts the curtains with vigorous yanks on the cord. A dusky light bathes the room. Outside, the sun is sinking below swathes of red cirrus into a calm, burnished sea. "How can you stare at those freaks on TV when you have God's own creation to look at?"

Artemisa pulls at the nurse's hand so that the two of them stand blocking his view of the television screen . Sarah hears him take a deep breath, as if he were preparing to speak. Instead, with a twitch of his thumb he raises the volume  to a sustained blare. "Both shoulders fractured in the accident," she nearly shouts. "He can't move his arms and hands except to turn on the TV. All fifty-four channels." She tries to tease a smile out of him. "He likes Univision and MTV because they have sexy girls, *verdad, viejo*?"

The man's gray eyes remain fixed on a corner of the tv.

"This is the night nurse, Carlitos. Se llama Sarah."

Carlos Valle finally shifts his gaze to the younger woman. She wears white slacks and a crisp white blouse, all very professional except for the top button left undone to reveal a speckling of light freckles in the V between her breasts.

"Buenos días, señor Valle." Sarah touches the inert hand on his lap.

Carlos presses the mute button and the room falls silent. "Días?" he frowns in mock confusion. "The *night* nurse says 'buenos días'? Buenos días at the end of the day, when the sun is setting?" He gestures with his head at the fading light over the ocean. "I wonder what the day nurse will say. I am confused as well as crippled."

Sarah blushes. She thinks back to her high school Spanish class, having known even then it would be useful. *"Buenas noches,"* she corrects herself. *"Cómo está usted, señor Valle?"* She expects him to answer, *Muy bien, gracias.* Or maybe, *Más o menos, gracias.* More or less okay. He nods listlessly, in response to what he considers a rhetorical question.

"You see, my dear?" Artemisa says clasping Sarah's hand. "He is not going to be an easy patient."

"We'll get along," she smiles.

"I can find someone else."

"We'll be just fine," she insists. "I'm glad for the chance to work nights. That way my boyfriend and I can be on the same schedule."

"Miss Jardine asked how you were, *querido*," she reminds her husband.

*"Estoy de la chingada,"* he finally says hoarsely, as if the effort has taken all the energy he has at this moment.

Artemisa turns toward the nurse apologetically. "It's a crude expression. It means he is in bad shape."

"Fucked up." Carlos Valle nods in agreement. He shuts his eyes.

He presses the volume control, and the TV set explodes in a clamor of voices that makes Artemisa wince. "We should leave him now. Sarah will sit just outside the door, Carlitos."

"Do you need anything right now, señor Valle?" The nurse asks, raising her voice above the din.

He turns off the set. "Accidente," he rasps.

The two women are heading for the door. "Sí Carlitos," Artemisa turns to him impatiently. "I've explained to Sarah that you broke your shoulders in an accident." Then she says to the nurse,

"Call him don Carlos. He will like that. It's what everyone called him in the government. Don Carlos Valle, Minister of Planeación and Desarrollo."

Carlos sighs impatiently. "*Ac-ci-den-te*," he says through gritted teeth. It takes a moment for his meaning to become clear. Meanwhile, he feels himself sinking into some primeval swamp, its vapors rising all about him.

*Los machos se aguantan*, they can hold it. He learned early on that he was not to let his body get the best of him. Not like the old men in the senate, who after a six-hour speech by the Presidente, not daring to show disrespect by excusing themselves, would leave puddles on the red leather armchairs.

In school, only sissies raised their hand in class to be excused. Justice was swift and public. Ten smacks of the ruler for losing control. Frequent infractors were made to wear diapers. It was all in the shaping of a young man, an *hombrecito*: We're training the leaders of tomorrow; your boys will make the grade. Parents agreed that some pain was beneficial.

Sarah is already moving toward Don Carlos. "I'll deal with it," she says, her eyes urging Artemisa to leave them. Carlos tries to wave the nurse away, but a searing pain starts at the point where neck meets collar bone and streaks down the length of his arm. If only she will leave him alone, surely he can put up with the pain to move his own body to the bathroom and pull down his own pants and twist his broken arms around to wipe his own ass.

***

The events leading to this pain remain vivid in Carlos Valle's mind. During lunch with Pedro and Betty Macías, his prostate the size of a mango was making him twitch in his chair with the overwhelming need to piss. "Con permiso," he said. With the unhurried dignity befitting the former Minister of Planeación and Desarollo, he walked to the men's room by the lobby.

The restroom, all soft lights and gleaming steel and porcelain, appeared to be deserted. A moment later, while waiting for some timid dribble, he became aware of two men at the urinals on either side of him. To his left stood a pair of black lizard-skin cowboy boots. He glimpsed a brass belt buckle in the shape of a steer's head. Of the man on his right, he saw part of his shirt, powder blue silk, shimmering under the ceiling lights. Their presence exuded a cloying lotion, dark Mexican cigarettes, warm urine foaming up in the bowl. Carlos fixed his gaze on the tiled wall before him. It would not do to provide an opening for the homosexuals rumored to hustle rich men in the better hotels.

"A ver, joven." The man's fingers gestured insistently. "Give me the Rolex, yes?"

There was some comfort in knowing he was being robbed rather than accosted. Still, the phony courtesy, the underlying sarcasm of addressing a seventy-year-old as joven, spoken in the calm unhurried tones of experienced thieves, all hinted at violence. Don Carlos held out his arm for the man to slide the watch from his wrist. It had been a gift from Artemisa to celebrate his first important post back in government. Carlos tried to steady his trembling hand which now felt unfamiliarly light.

The one to his right breathed into his ear, "*A mí me das la lana, viejo.*" He would take his money. There was some humor here, one of them calling him *joven* and the other *viejo*, the latter tinged with affection: *Hola, viejo, que tal estas?* He was grateful for any token of regard. The reach for his wallet was interrupted by a stinging slap on his hand. Two fingers sneaked like pincers into his pocket and withdrew the billfold. Carlos did not feel a thing. The man removed a wad of fifties and hundreds, plus the credit cards, then dropped the wallet into the urinal.

Carlos hoped they were finished. "*Muchísimas gracias, Señor Ministro Don Carlos Valle,*" the Rolex thief said expansively. "What a surprise to run into you like this, *verdad?*"

"*Qué chico es el mundo,*" his partner agreed.

A small world, indeed, Carlos thought—the exile zone. He was not surprised that they had recognized him from the public revelations of bribery and theft that so many years later still seemed so recent. He wanted to see their faces before they fled; perhaps he would recognize them as well. He was turning toward the man on his right when he felt a sharp pain on his shins as his legs were kicked back, causing him to fall like a defeated chess king at a flick of the winner's finger. Black and white marble tiles rushed up. He saw the lip of the urinal coming toward his face, centering on the underside of his nose. He jerked his head back as cool porcelain brushed his skin. He reached down with his hands to break the fall. Instead, he heard his shoulders crack under the weight of his body.

He thought it best to be still until the sound of the closing door signaled that his assailants had walked away. When he did try to get up, the pain screaming from his shoulders made any movement impossible. He told himself to relax, that someone would be coming into the men's room at any moment. He wanted to zip up his fly. He didn't like the idea of being discovered on the bathroom floor, his pito sticking out, urine on his pants. He was relieved it was Artemisa who found him.

\*\*\*

Sarah Jardine buckles a leather harness around her patient's waist. "You have to let me know when you need to go, Don Carlos. You mustn't be shy with me." She curls the straps around her hands and easily pulls him from the chair onto his feet. She marvels at how small he is, yet handsome, with a large well-sculpted head, an expressive face and gray wavy hair that he wears brushed straight back. When seated, holding his head erect, he appears taller than he is. Together, her hand still clutching the belt strap, they take tentative steps down the hall toward the bathroom.

"You're a strong girl," he smiles. "The nurse during the day is bigger but she has more trouble getting me off the chair."

"It's all technique," Sarah says confidently. Yet, after six years of experience she's still surprised at her equanimity when helping weak, fragile patients clean their private places. Like wiping a baby's butt, she was told in nursing school. But babies were objects, not yet persons. The eyes of the old would stare out at her, sometimes welling up with tears of anger and shame. Sarah pulls don Carlos' fine robe off his shoulders, verifies that it's clean and hangs it on a hook. Then she lowers him onto the toilet seat and, kneeling on the floor, pulls off his soiled pajama pants.

"It was an accident."

"No excuses, don Carlos," she says gently. "The next time, you will tell me in time. Sí?"

He nods, anxious to finish the discussion, while she stands at the sink washing her hands. "You don't wear gloves," he says when she begins to sponge him. "The other nurse puts on rubber gloves first thing."

***

At eight, the table is set. "You will eat dinner with us," Artemisa has told Sarah. "It will be important to Carlitos that we carry on our way of life, *verdad, querido?*" Don Carlos nods from the opposite end of the long mahogany table.

Violets flanked by two silver candlesticks serve as a centerpiece. "We have much to celebrate," Artemisa insists, raising her own glass. "Our family always has champagne when there is something to be glad for. And today, we have cause to be happy that, with the help of such a gracious nurse as Miss Jardine, Carlitos is on the way to recovery."

Sarah sits to Don Carlos's right. In front of him, there is a glass of champagne and a plate of baked fish, soft green beans and mashed potatoes. She cuts small pieces and raises the fork to his mouth. After every couple of bites she touches a corner of the napkin to his lips. She makes sure her touch is gentle. She has seen other nurses, and wives too, spooning, dabbing, wiping mechanically, forgetting that the mouth

66

they feed is attached to a person's face. At Artemisa's insistence, Sarah raises the champagne to his lips; Don Carlos with his drooping eyelids and nodding head seems to grow more relaxed with every sip, the combination of Vicodin and Tattinger cloaking his pain in shadows.

Artemisa works to keep conversation flowing. "It's unusual for a young woman to want to work nights. It must be terrible for your social life."

"I don't socialize so much, señora."

"There must be a young man in your life," Artemisa says.

"Yes. His name is Ted."

"A nice doctor, perhaps?"

"He cures computers."

"Very modern. Have some more mashed potatoes," she says, pushing the platter in her direction. "I'm sorry we are having such bland food, but it is for Carlitos' digestion. Two years ago, you would have come for dinner and thought we were in Mexico. Even here in California, in our voluntary but necessary exile, we could eat like back home. Mole. Nopalitos. *Huachinango a la veracruzana.* Flan for dessert. Carlitos loves his flan, the sweeter the better, the more eggs the richer. Some day while you're here, we'll have flan. And we will let Carlitos have some, *verdad, querido*?" She falls silent. Carlos' head has fallen forward, his shoulders are slumped, his eyes closed. He breathes slowly, rhythmically.

"I'd better get him to bed."

"Come back, querida,' Artemisa says. "We are just now getting acquainted."

When Sarah returns, Artemisa lingers at the table, sipping the last of her coffee. "I wait until he has gone to sleep before I take my coffee," she says. "I seem to be truly awake only when he's asleep." She pours some for Sarah. "I don't suppose that is a very nice confession."

Sarah tries to shrug off any need to comment.

"At any rate, I am so glad you are with us. You are an excellent nurse."

"Thank you, señora."

Artemisa reaches out to touch Sarah's hand. Reflexively, Sarah starts to clasp the older woman's hand, when she feels on her palm the texture of a crisply folded bill. "Don't look at it now," Artemisa says. "It's a small gift."

Sarah opens her hand anyway and sees $100. "I don't know what this is for." She places it on the table in front of Artemisa.

"Your patient, Don Carlos, might present some special difficulties." Artemisa smiles sympathetically. "He is not always on his best behavior."

"Really, señora. It's my job to take care of problems."

"You have to understand, dear. I love my Carlitos. His needs are not to be considered problems. Be kind to him," she added, taking the bill and pressing it again to Sarah's hand. "We can all be kind to each other."

\*\*\*

The one a.m. Vicodin will shut the door on the pain once again. Until then the slightest movement and unexpected pressure upon either of his shoulders cracks the door open and hoarse moans rush out with renewed fury. Carlos bites down on a corner of the bedsheet and shuts his eyes against the pain. While he's awake, he won't make a sound. That is his resolution, to handle himself with dignity. It's only in the depths of sleep that, unguarded, the soft whimpering comes out. When señorita Jardine comes into his room to check on his posture or give him medication, he wonders how she knows to come in at that moment. He thinks she is psychic. Bruja, he calls her in his mind.

When Sarah hears Carlos complain she gives him the pill with a cup of warm milk. She washes his face with a cool towel. She helps him sit up and runs her fingernails up and down his back. He tells her to do it more vigorously because his dry skin feels if it were crawling with ants. She asks him how he's feeling, how goes the pain. He doesn't tell her that the sensation of her nails leaving parallel streaks from the back of his neck to his waist has given him an erection.

*** 

Carlos Valle was thirty when he fell in love with Artemisa. He had the strong jawline and thick wavy hair that she liked in men. In photographs his head looked like it belonged to a taller man. In person he was chubby and his arms were so short he had to have a tailor shorten the sleeves of his new shirts. He was painfully aware of his shortcomings. He feared that the size of his penis would be insufficient for a tall woman like Artemisa. When he confessed his love for her, she asked him what he aspired to in life. It was a serious, definitive question; she had not yet married because the men who courted her were all the type to be satisfied with very little; a good government position, to be obtained through her family's connections. It was not enough for Artemisa. "You have to know your destiny," she challenged Carlos.

"I'm going to accomplish great things for Mexico," he boasted. "We will travel the world, meet the Pope and the Shah and García Marquez. Our friends will be poets and artists and film stars."

They were having this conversation at two in the morning in a dark corner of the top floor terrace of the Hotel Majestic during the *noche del grito*, the Mexican Independence Day gala. The ballroom inside was crowded with preening banking and government functionaries, the men in black, the women wearing stiff, bell-shaped taffeta dresses in purple and mauve and lapis. They were all pleased to be thrown together in this celebration, to recognize each other, to reaffirm their status. Giddy from champagne and cognac and cuba libras, they'd lined up and were doing a cute dance from Europe, the Macarena.

Outside, the night sky was tattooed with fireworks. In the Zócalo below people packed the square, cheering and yelling *Viva México*. Artemisa stood very close to Carlos. He could smell a heady scent from her spicy skin, moist from the dancing. He knew with absolute certainty that the next few seconds were going to be like jumping off the roof of the Hotel Majestic. There would be no clawing his way back. Everything about this moment had been written for him, and all he could do was speak the words that came to his head and watch himself open a door that had been awaiting his arrival since birth. He couldn't understand how all around them people could just go off and act like children when at this very moment, he and Artemisa were dying to their former selves.

Taller than Carlos by six inches, she discreetly pressed against him, lowered the bodice of her dress and bared a pale generous breast for him to touch. He stared at it in disbelief and thought of the plump swell of a pear, the glistening flesh of a guanabana, a mound of whipped cream with chopped nuts. She pulled Carlos down by the back of his head and his mouth opened reflexively.

"*Trato hecho*," she breathed out a long sigh over the top of his head. "It's a deal, *querido*."

\*\*\*

In the tender morning light, Artemisa leans over the edge of the terrace and breathes in the cool air. The slope of her garden, bursting with hyacinths and roses, leads her gaze to the crashing breakers at the end of a drop-off. This is her favorite time. The shore below emerges from under a layer of mist that leaves a dewy patina on every surface. In a few hours the sun will be burning through the moisture. But now, while the day is gray and silent, its sounds are somehow muffled by the fog so that the roar of the occasional car, the stray radio broadcast, the random child's cry, seem distant. Even the sounds inside the house as the new nurse prepares Carlos for his bath after the long night, their voices first, then his small cries of pain, the roar of water, all sound distant. It's a comforting sensation, the feeling that her problems have receded to some dim horizon.

This morning, she has her coffee and pastry at a wrought-iron table on the patio. The coffee is from the Chiapas highlands and the croissant from Le Grand Epicure, her favorite bakery in the village. At an outrageous $4.75 each, every bite must be attended to. Moment by moment, as the buttery flakes dissolve in her mouth, she realizes that for the past few years her husband has been in retreat. First, he surrendered their bedroom to her. He was starting to smell like an old man, she claimed. The cheap Mexican cigarettes that he liked, the lavender brilliantine for his slicked down hair, the strong menthol drops for his night coughs. Everything you eat is seeping out through your pores in the night, she accused him. You are sweating lard and chiles, beans and cheese and fermenting corn meal. Your pants smell.

Later, he started falling asleep in the living room while reading his Mexican newspapers or in the middle of conversations, slumping down like a melting candle, his head falling to one side, his breathing long and heavy. She managed to coax him into spending his days in the sitting room by his bedroom. The two small rooms became Carlos' own exile zone. He could tumble from the recliner chair to the bed for a quick nap. Then he could go from the bed to the small writing desk for his middle-of-the-night sessions with the eternal writing of his *memorias*.

Artemisa was living life to the fullest. Every day, she would make an occasion of stopping by to see him. She wore short skirts and revealing blouses, lacy black stockings, high heels, her features enlivened with lipstick, eyebrow pencil, and rouge.

"*Pareces puta*," he would say.

"Es puro show." She would laugh, so he wouldn't worry.

Sometimes her visit would be in the evening, and they would have a *merienda* like in Mexico, coffee with milk and pan dulce. Ignoring these small efforts, he complained that the Mexican pastries were too rich, that they gave him heartburn.

"Too rich, too salty, too sweet, too much," she mimicked him. "Enjoy life, *viejo*."

"*Si, querida*," he would say without much conviction. Then he would glance at his watch, check the TV Guide, and press the remote to his favorite shows on the Spanish channels.

"A group of us is going out to dinner," she would say then.

Maybe, if she mentioned their friends Betty and Pedro Macías, he might join in; he enjoyed looking at Betty. Ordinarily, he wouldn't be interested.

"Chinese tonight, with the widows," she might inform him apologetically. "I'll bring you the egg rolls with hot mustard that you like."

"If they're not too greasy," he would reply.

\*\*\*

This is the moment Carlos dreads. His pear-shaped body stands under the shower, face directed toward the spray, hands dangling somewhere just below his navel. Sarah Jardine touches him wherever he cannot reach. She runs a washcloth along his shoulders and arms, down his back and buttocks. She is thorough. He feels her parting his ass cheeks, rubbing the soapy cloth into his anus, coaxing his thighs apart so she can cross to his testicles, then facing him, swirling around his chest a descending spiral from his chest and midriff down his belly to his shrunken, fearful penis. This penis doesn't want to offend; it disregards its own appetites out of civility, or fear.

To dry him Sarah sits on the edge of the bathtub and runs a towel up and down his legs from his calves to his back. She has him raise one foot to her lap then the other. The touch of the soft terrycloth on his toes, along the sole, up the ankle, leaps with an unexpected shiver of pleasure at the back of his neck, as if his feet and head were linked by secret threads. He forces his mind to think of other things to pull himself out of the moment's incipient sensuality: picking out the Pleiades out of the night sky, recalling the Buendía family tree in *Cien Años de Soledad*, following soccer with squat brown men with thighs like logs chasing after a ball.

There are distractions to the distraction. A sweet dark smell rises from the young woman's thick curls. He cannot think of anything else. There are rules about this. You shall not desire any woman younger than your daughter, nor play with the help, nor humiliate yourself by starting what you know you can't finish.

"That's enough," he says impatiently.

"Are you feeling pain?" She pulls away for a moment. "I can't let you dress while you're still wet."

He shakes his head, unable for the moment to say what he's thinking. "Not being able to manage by myself," he begins. "It makes me feel like a baby."

She resumes drying him, moving the plush fabric lightly down the backs of his legs, to his ankles, the tops of his feet. "No, Don Carlos, don't feel like a baby," she says. "Feel like a king."

"I'm not sure I remember how."

Carlos sees the blurry outlines of his body reflected in the steamy bathroom mirror and looks away quickly. He is ashamed of his body, all curves and quivering mounds, from his pendulous breasts to his protruding belly, soft flesh rolling down from below his chest to his groin and around to his hips grown wide and shapeless like an old woman's.

Sarah continues to rub down his legs. "It takes a special talent to enjoy being a king," she says.

"I seem to be out of practice."

She drapes a terrycloth robe around his shoulders and ties it snugly around his waist. She slips her fingers under the belt to steady him and walks beside him down the hallway and into the bedroom. She closes the door behind her.

"A king asks for whatever he wants," he says.

"That's what being a king is all about," she smiles.

"It would be humiliating for the king to be turned down. It would mean that the king had no power," he adds, while she stands in front of him, holding a pair of boxer shorts for him to step into. "I don't even have the power to touch myself." Her face reveals nothing as she kneels on the carpet and parts the folds of the robe so he can step into the shorts. He tries to move his hands down lower on his belly but the pain shoots back up into his shoulders.

"Sit down, Don Carlos," she says, putting the shorts aside and helping him sit on the edge of the bed. She takes a bottle of skin lotion from the nightstand, and squeezes some onto her palms. She rubs it in circles along his lower abdomen and up and down the insides of his thighs.

"How long since you've been touched like this?" she asks, so softly he's not sure he's heard her. He starts to ask her to repeat, but suspects he's been given only one chance. Her question reminds him of a priest asking when he's had his last confession. It's been three weeks, Father. Or three years. That is the first sin, the time he has gone without absolution. He searches for a precise answer, as if there were one particular moment he would recall as the beginning of the end of Artemisa's desire for him.

"Dear girl," he says. "There are things that must be kept private in the exile zone."

# Yolanda by Day

Every day, all over the country, Babies are shaken into silence, dropped, squashed and tickled to hysterics, hung by their feet, or tossed in the air like volleyballs. Infants are allowed to cry themselves blue while Nannies try on your clothes, dance to your system, sample your pills, and yes, play with your toys. Nannies have been known to turn tricks out of homes in Westwood, deal meth and worse through the mail slot in your front door. One Nanny and her boyfriend even took Baby along on a spree of convenience-store robberies. (www.watchthatnanny.com)

My wife and I nodded our emphatic agreement. We felt vulnerable to the awful things likely to happen when we leave Baby with Stranger. The Watch-That-Nanny sales pitch preys on guilt, confronting Working Mom with her self-serving, career-centered, money-grubbing priorities. Utterly obvious: We bought.

Naturally, if any of us had the choice, we would all be perfect parents, dedicated 24/7 to our Baby. (www. watchthatnanny.com)

Staying home with Baby Pippa (Philippa in honor of her grandfather Phillip "Pip" Paxton) was not an option. The march of professional advancement goes on, leaving the stragglers to eat corporate dust. Parental leave options make us vulnerable to opportunistic, backstabbing colleagues. So, after six weeks, it's back to Cubicle City where the New Mom is sales promotion manager at a major manufacturer of modular office space. The New Dad, making a lot more money and precariously ensconced on an upper rung of the ladder, didn't skip a day on account of Baby Pippa.

> Fortunately, you have found a Nanny who is actually
> part Angel. (www.watchthatnanny.com)

After interviewing a dozen applicants, I persuaded my wife that Yolanda Campos, originally of Uruapan, Michoacán, now of East LA, was the perfect Nanny for Baby Pippa: Yolanda projected self-assurance and serenity beyond her youth. I anticipated her cooing Spanish endearments and singing Mexican lullabies to Baby Pippa, thus starting her on the road to multiculturalism.

I did not mention how her dark, flickering eyes momentarily locked on mine. Or how a smile appeared slyly when she sensed me glancing at the upper swell of her breasts. Could it be that she was responding to my interest, even a little? A point in her favor. All the time, while these small sparks were flying, my wife was focusing on her half-page resumé and letter of recommendation from her previous job at Uncle Alfonso's Burrito Barn.

> But, there is no such thing as a perfect jewel in
> Nannydom, is there? (www.watchthatnanny.com)

My wife did not think Yolanda was as terrific as I did. She said she was too young (19?), and way too Latina: the pompadoured hair, the navel ring and the big gold cross burrowed in her cleavage. What did some Vida Loca girl know about being responsible with an infant?

I pointed out that childcare is an ancestral tradition in Yolanda's culture. Girls as young as ten take care of baby siblings. It's in their DNA.

To be honest, and inspired by the Watch That Nanny, Inc. sales pitch, we decided that Yolanda would, in fact, be supervised ten hours a day with our child, in our apartment, with our stuff. The worms of distrust had wriggled their way into our head. A little benign surveillance would let us be a fly on the wall.

> At Watch that Nanny, Inc, our motto is: What you don't see can hurt...your precious Baby. (www.watchthatnanny.com)

We had the right to spy. The welfare of our child was at stake. Nothing less than the Double-Eye System would do: one tiny camera in a fake lamp on top of the television, another one in the kitchen peeking out from inside a wall clock. This was done based on research that shows that the average Nanny spends most of her time either eating or watching TV. If she wasn't within range, we could only assume she was in the bathroom (excusable) or in our bedroom (alarming). The system was automatic. We'd turn on a switch just before Yolanda showed up in the morning, and the digital recorder in a closet would start humming.

> No, it's not an invasion of Nanny's privacy. Employers have a right to protect precious belongings from their employees. (www.watchthatnanny.com)

I couldn't wait to check the results the first day. We gave Baby Pippa her bath, her bottle, her hugs and snuggles. After putting her to bed we sat down for the evening's entertainment with a feast of Peking Palace #36, #42, and #8 with extra egg roll. In the surprisingly sharp picture, we could see Yolanda stretched out on the couch, Baby Pippa a bundle cuddled on her lap, like a cat or a teddy bear. The sound recording crackled with Univision's Buenos Días América and Yolanda's sweet lullabies.

We fast-forwarded. Occasionally Yolanda would eerily aim the remote at us through the concealed camera lens, as if she could see *us* watching *her*. When she walked to the kitchen, a motion detector switched on that camera, and we saw her taking the formula bottle out of the microwave, shaking a few drops on her wrist, then flicking her tongue out to lick them off her skin.

A moment later she was back in the living room. She expertly nestled Baby Pippa against her bosom while feeding her. Even though we couldn't see Baby Pippa's face, we were reassured by the happy sounds of her gurgling and sucking.

After a while, Yolanda lay Baby Pippa across her shoulder, and patted her back a couple of times until we heard a loud burp. Oh, how we chuckled, my wife and I. Night after night, watching the tape was like visiting with Baby Pippa, being part of her day. We could imagine her contented face as she spit out a dribble of curdled milk. Yolanda was doing a fine job. We kept fast forwarding looking for action: Yolanda standing, swaying back and forth with Baby Pippa on her hip. Yolanda putting Baby Pippa in her crib. Yolanda making herself nachos in the microwave. Yolanda eating said nachos in front of the kitchen camera. I enjoyed watching Yolanda move about. She carried her body with grace that was downright poetic.

> We store the signal from your recorder in our web site.
> You will confirm suspicions or have evidence in case of
> any incident. (www.watchthatnanny.com)

We also watched because we were sure we were going to catch Yolanda doing something amusing. We got a small kick looking at her without her knowledge. We fast-forwarded to her answering the phone or going to the door when the mailman came. But outside of the buzz I derived from seeing her stretch or yawn or primp in front of the mirror, there was little action. Occasionally, she did a quick dance to the music from the TV. It was a fine little move, just a shimmy of her shoulders and a wiggle of her hips. It kept me rewinding and looking at it over and over until my wife decided I had gone beyond the bounds of normal voyeurism.

> Some of our clients find that observing their Nanny
> during unguarded moments provides valuable insights
> into human behavior. (www.watchthatnanny.com)

I expect young, single people to maintain an active telephone life, but Yolanda did not make or receive calls. Perhaps she was avoiding someone, using our house and Baby Pippa as a kind of screen, to conveniently stay out of sight all day long. I envisioned her hiding from her abusive Uncle Alfonso the burrito man, in hassles with the Chavas Locas gang, or in debt to a ring of smuggling coyotes. I was glad to offer her some protection.

Yolanda feeding a bottle to Baby Pippa or Yolanda making a sandwich for herself were reliably amusing. I learned to fast-forward through the long stretches of inactivity, to seek out the familiar gestures of her hand brushing stray hair from her face or, in a reflexive act of modesty, the tug at the hem of her little skirt in front of the mirror.

My wife soon lost interest. The day's tapes were banished from prime-time and relegated to the late-late show. Watching the nanny tapes during my bouts of two a.m. insomnia helped me relax. I would sit in our dark living room with the sound off, scanning the jerky images until Yolanda would lean over a restless Baby Pippa and sing her some Spanish ditty and shake a rattle in a really cute way. Then she would settle back down on the couch, with Baby Pippa in her arms, and both of us, Baby and Daddy would grow drowsy.

> It's better not to grow attached to your Nanny, because
> revelations from the surveillance system might
> necessitate her dismissal. (www.watchthatnanny.com)

Try talking to Baby Pippa about not getting attached. Her first spitty little grins were for Yolanda when, upon arriving in the morning, she picked her up and held her to her breast. At the end of the day, Baby Pippa would break into anguished screams when Yolanda tried to hand her to me or her mom. We were clearly inadequate replacements.

Even with all the turmoil of Baby Pippa crying and our scrambling for the exact change for her bus fare, I would take great care to look at Yolanda and remember the details of her look on a particular night. The halter top and leather skirt, or the T-shirt with the rhinestone butterfly and the skinny jeans and tall blue platforms that matched her toenails. I would note her color of eye shadow that day, the shade of lipstick, the gloss of her nails, plus the rings, studs and posts that decorated her fingers, ears, toes, navel. Yolanda loved big vibrant colors. She was particularly fond of pink and turquoise and purple which she played off against her black leather skirts and indigo jeans.

My wife thought Yolanda dressed slutty. To me, she looked like a particularly festive sort of angel, albeit one with a dangerous appeal. The sharper my memory of her, the clearer the picture that came through the video.

> The strategic placement of small temptations can reveal
> a Nanny's character before it becomes a problem.
> (www.watchthatnanny.com)

It was my wife's idea to place a silver dish with an exact number of Godiva chocolates on top of the TV set. The Character Test, as my wife called it, reignited her interest in the tapes. My wife expected Yolanda to yield; I knew she would resist.

We put Baby Pippa to bed and settled ourselves on the couch, the candy dish between us. For the first couple of hours during the morning, Yolanda was busy doing the normal Nanny things with Baby Pippa, and even after she glanced at the candy dish, there was not even a moment's pause to consider taking one. But, as my wife pointed out, she had seen them; the knowledge would linger in her mind. Mexicans, after all, loved chocolate, had invented chocolate, it was in their DNA to grab chocolate the way Americans grab potato chips. The Nanny would surrender to her sweet tooth and her larcenous nature. I snapped that she was reducing cultural stereotypes to the pseudo scientific determinism of genetic mumbo jumbo. She should be ashamed.

What the hell was I talking about? she countered. I was a sneaky voyeur. She had a point and it stung. I didn't say anything until the end of the recording. Yolanda had glanced at the chocolates a couple of times in the morning, followed by a lingering gaze around three p.m. In the end, she had left them untouched. How was that for character, I said.

Our Nanny was a tough little sprite. I was proud of her. I may be a voyeur, I thought, but only in the way a bird watcher or a star gazer is a voyeur, one filled with wonder and admiration. I tried not to gloat when my wife went to bed feeling miffed. I stayed up and watched. Nothing much happened, except that Yolanda for the first time looked at the camera hidden behind the lamp, and smiled. I thought that maybe she had seen the lens.

> The Nanny does not expect a personal relationship with the Parents. Only with the Baby. This distance will be helpful in case of a problem. (www.watchthatnanny. com)

The day after the Candy Test, I mentioned to Yolanda, as I was leaving for work, that there were some nice chocolates in the bowl and that she could, of course, help herself. That evening there were two moments when Yolanda walked up to the candy dish, and after careful consideration of the contents, took one and bit into it with her pretty teeth. She stood in front of the camera, as if lost in the sensation of chocolate slowly melting in the warmth of her mouth. Again, I wondered for a moment if she was making a point of staring at me, our snooping discovered.

> Some Nannies do not mind taking on extra chores, such as doing breakfast dishes, a load of laundry, or answering the phone. It makes their day more interesting, especially if they are caring for infants. (www.watchthatnanny.com)

I started ringing our home number for the pleasure of seeing Yolanda rise from the sofa and walk to the phone. She would say, Hello, wait a few moments, and then I would hang up. I couldn't very well say I had called just to hear her throaty voice or watch her sexy walk, one hip jutting out as a perch for Baby Pippa. I took to staying on the line, breathing softly. Not in an alarming manner, I hoped, but as anybody would normally breathe. This kept her standing with the phone a little longer, a fist on her waist, her voice going Hello, Hola, Bueno. And then one day, Fuck you, pendejo. Sure, I had it coming. I had crossed an important line, from concerned observer to active contaminator of the surveillance environment. It took a couple of days for the weirdness to go away. After that, I was able to freely indulge my obsession.

I did not tell my wife I was doing this. By now she had given up watching the recordings altogether, but my insomnia, further awakened by remorse, had gotten worse.

> The Nanny will never become a member of your family.
> Eventually the cord to your Baby will be cut. (www.
> watchthatnanny.com)

My wife was back in full swing at Cubicle City. She had put her career in high gear. I thought there was a nice irony in her exalting the Cubicle City modular office space systems, while all the time she was aiming for a real office with walls to the ceiling, a door, and a window. More and more often, she called to tell me she had to work late. I was not one to stand in way of her success; it was up to me to get home in time to relieve the Nanny.

I would often pretend to search around for bus fare in order to keep up a stream of chit chat with Yolanda. I would ask her how their day had gone, hers and Baby Pippa's. I would make sure we were standing in camera range. She would still be holding Baby Pippa cooing and asking her in Spanish baby talk if *la bebita* had been good. If *la bebita* was glad to see her *papacito*. If *la bebita* would miss her nana.

I found myself basking in the loving aura that surrounded Yolanda and Baby Pippa. If I stood close enough to the two of them, ostensibly to gaze down on the Baby's fuzzy pate and wrinkled face, but also close enough to feel the faint brush of Yolanda's shoulder and smell the spicy fragrance of her exuberant hair, then the aura enveloped me as well. The moment would end with Yolanda thrusting Baby Pippa into my arms; she had to make three bus connections to East LA.

> You can be sued by your Nanny! We can insure you against personal injury from slippery floors, unknown assailants, faulty wiring, fires, mudslides, and claims of sexual harassment arising from misinterpreted touching and careless banter. (www.watchthatnanny.com)

One evening Yolanda was picking up the scattered toys from her play session with Baby Pippa, and I followed along while she handed me a rattle, a plush skunk, a sticky tennis ball and a book with cloth pages. After I put the stuff inside Baby Pippa's toy box, I gave Yolanda her bus fare. She looked at the money suspiciously and thanked me politely but with little joy. She appeared to be in a hurry. I, on the other hand, went to some lengths to slow her down. I asked her questions about what her plans were for the weekend (dancing), how her night school was going (boring), what she enjoyed doing with her friends (shopping).

I had been standing between her and the door, and all the time I knew I was being stupid, that I couldn't expect her to stay and chat with me, just because I had given her ten dollars for the bus. Oh, what a tremendous effort it took not to cop a subtle feel when she finally slipped past me, brushing against me and leaving me drunk with the invisible eddies of her familiar soapy fragrance.

> Don't get involved. Nannies have messy lives that are best left outside, before Nanny enters your home and engages your Baby. (www.watchthatnanny.com)

I didn't realize how stupidly I'd behaved until I saw the whole thing on tape that night. There I was, bobbing about like some teenager, arms twitching at my side, hands restlessly fingering the seams in my pants to keep from clutching the girl before me.

I could see Yolanda's back on the tape, her shoulders shuddering in an irritated sigh. Her voice was edged with apprehension. After weeks of courting her with my eyes I was experiencing the sting of her rejection. It had been stupid not to turn off the recorder. Talk about evidence singling me out as a potential, if not already de facto, harasser. That did not prevent me, in the throes of my two-a.m. restlessness, from replaying the scene a half dozen times.

She'd been somewhat surprised, possibly intimidated by my overbearing presence. In retrospect, the moment could not be construed yet as an attempted seduction. My interest had been somewhat paternal, which was to be expected of older, wealthy white people who took an interest in disadvantaged youths. Considering what I realize now was the strength of my desire for Yolanda, I was proud of my restraint. All I had done, really, was hover about clumsily and utter pathetic conversational gambits. Hardly a crime.

> It's not uncommon to want the same level of affection that the Nanny lavishes on the Baby to be spread to the Parents. Attention Daddy: You won't be the first guy who wrecked his life because he lusted after Baby's Nanny. (www.watchthatnanny.com)

I was, of course, perfectly justified in calling my home number, ostensibly to see how things were going with Baby Pippa. I made up other excuses. To ask if a Mr. So-and-So had tried to reach me at home. To let Yolanda know that my wife and I would be late. Or to ask if Baby Pippa's sniffles were better. I could tell Yolanda was uncertain about these calls. But she would answer politely, and then chat for a minute about what Baby Pippa was doing. She was not warming up to me. One night, I cringed when I saw her shake her head and flip me the finger after slamming the phone. Things were not improving between us.

A clever Nanny could spot the camera—and not let on!
(www.watchthatnanny.com)

I don't know when Yolanda noticed the camera, first the one on the TV, then two days later the one in the kitchen. An early sign was her spending more and more time out of the lens' range. She would lie prone on the carpet while playing with Baby Pippa, and all I'd see was the top of her head. Eventually, she placed her backpack squarely against the lamp with the camera. The tape showed seven hours of black! Yet the sounds coming from the room were tantalizing—Yolanda cooing, making baby talk and singing Mexican nursery rhymes —a la *ruru nena, duérmase mi bien*. One time when out of view, I heard her talking with Baby Pippa about how hot it was and how nice it would feel for both la bebita and la nana to take their clothes off. Oh, sí, sí, to take a cool shower and run around naked. (Giggling!) There was the sound of water running from the bathroom. Meanwhile, as the tape rolled dark, my wife slept. Baby Pippa slept. I lay awake and prayed: Oh, God, I whispered, please let me *see*.

You can change the location of the camera without Nanny realizing it. Call for our re-installation advice!
(www.watchthatnanny.com)

There you go, Señorita Yolanda. I've outsmarted you. I feel this puts our relationship on a new, lightly adversarial level. There's an undeniable familiarity in this You-versus-Me situation that makes me think of Yolanda as a complex person, not the shy señorita that came to interview only three months ago. This new Yolanda is not without her flaws and ticks, but as we get to know each other, personal interaction is raised to a new level.

The new camera is waterproof and follows her at a wide angle from inside the turret of a clever aquarium sea castle. Oh, how she loves to sit in front of the glass and point out for the delight of Baby Pippa the guppies and gold-finned blippos, the azure zentians and the black-and-orange zebrafish cavorting and having fun.

For days now, Yolanda has been moving about the apartment quite freely, not realizing that the lens she covered on top of the TV is now a decoy for the new all-seeing eye that stalks her. She's been Baby Pippa's Nanny for about six months, and it's nice seeing her get comfortable in our home. I fear that she knows more than I realize about my wife and me. There are telltale signs that she's been inside our closets, opened drawers, peeked into medicine cabinets. Ah, the little traviesa scamp.

But see? It works both ways. Getting to know you, getting to know all about you...Like this guy Francisco that has started calling her cell. I can't tell from Yolanda's monosyllables of the yes and no variety, with occasional agitated bursts in Spanish, whether he's a boyfriend or something less happy than that. Sometimes when the phone beeps she doesn't answer. I have her number and call with id off. Would she be surprised to hear my voice if she picked up? Whatever rapport I might have developed with Yolanda washed out once she learned I'm a sneak.

> You must impress on your Nanny that her social life
> is to be put on hold while she is giving her undivided
> attention to your Baby. (www.watchthatnanny.com)

Social life? Nobody has a social life anymore. Not the Nanny, not the Parents. My wife and I cuddle up to the Teletubbies and Barney. Our socializing happens on Facebook now, as we struggle to stay in touch with old friends. They don't call us as dependably as they used to. You should hear us carry on and on with Baby Pippa this and Baby Pippa that.

We go to bed at ten, pretty much exhausted. We hardly touch anymore. Then I get up at 2:00 to watch Yolanda on the day's video. I get to be part of her life during the ten hours she takes our place with Baby Pippa. It's strictly a one-way thing, but I do wonder if she suspects I've outsmarted her. I like to think that her behavior during the day has become purposeful just in case I am watching.

One day, after Baby Pippa has grown into a young woman and Yolanda comes back for a visit, I fantasize confessing to all my snooping. I will be a divorced old goat by then, and she will be married and have kids of her own, and I will say, Yolanda, you were the highpoint of my sleepless nights. And there will be that sly grin momentarily shaping her pretty mouth, and I will know that she knew.

Watch for signs that your Nanny may be indulging secret vices. Vigilance is all. (www.watchthatnanny.com)

Yolanda's dark side came as a surprise. Considering I was the one watching her every night, well, call me naive. My wife, on the other hand, assured me she'd always picked up a strange vibe from her, a guilty lowering of the eyes, an evasive answer to a simple question.

I could've fired Yolanda the moment she figured out she was being watched and covered the cameras. Instead, I became her opponent in this new game that had evolved between us. I was sure I had outsmarted her with the new lens placements.

I was not facing the new truth about her, even after I figured out, watching the tape, that the cigarette she was smoking right there with Baby Pippa on her lap was possibly marijuana. Or that my wife wondered who had been through her lingerie drawer. I thought I could smell Yolanda's aggressive perfume on my wife's nightie, but I chose not to say anything. By then, my consuming interest in Yolanda, though not yet quite an obsession, had driven me into some private corner where my wife sensed she was not welcome.

Finally, there was no doubt that I saw this Francisco guy actually show up at the door, the two of them giggling and tousling as she tried halfheartedly to shove him back out and he managed to come in anyway. He finally cornered her and pressed a kiss on her mouth. Surprisingly, she let her arms fall at her side and she stopped trying to push him away and kissed him back, right in front of the aquarium.

Was it to torture me? The two couldn't stop groping. And then she stepped out of her little skirt and shrugged off her T-shirt while the guy kicked off his shoes and dropped his pants. She moved Baby Pippa aside and they had a go on the living room sofa. It was all on the tape, and I realized that the spot where I was sitting was the exact spot where Yolanda's creamy brown ass had lain under the onslaught of that brute, Francisco. I went back to that scene a dozen times.

> A Nanny must be made to realize that your life is not
> her life. Your things are not her things. Your Baby is not
> her Baby. (www.watchthatnanny.com)

Meanwhile, the warning signs piled up: The telltale rummaging in my wife's lingerie drawer. An occasional beer missing from the fridge. A sprinkling of weed on the carpet. Francisco came more often and stayed longer. I considered adding an additional camera when I suspected that they were going into the bedroom.

Afterwards, he'd reappear in the living room, I could swear in my terrycloth bathrobe, hair slicked back, possibly wet from the shower. Yolanda would sit on the couch and watch TV with Baby Pippa gurgling happily between them. They would both play with our Baby, tossing her up and down, eliciting manic laughter and shrieks of pure delight.

The next day was a heart breaker. I called with one of my lame excuses. I was hoping she would get up from the bed and go bouncety-bouncety straight to the phone. Instead, a man's voice answered. I mumbled something about a wrong number. I was about to try again, when I realized that of course I had the number right; I've got "Home" on my office speed dial.

I immediately called my wife and told her we had to fire Yolanda. She said it was about time, that she thought I had fallen in love with her or something. I went ha, ha, but I know I sounded fake. To prove her wrong, I would do the deed. I withdrew enough cash to cover a week's salary plus some severance pay. I'd show up early, so she would not be expecting me. If her boyfriend was there, I would act shocked and tell them both to leave without any money at all.

> Call our Toll-Free Number at the first sign of an emergency. We will notify the proper authorities: INS, EMS, LAPD, FBI, DTSS, CPD, etc. (www. watchthatnanny.com)

I stood at our front door a full hour before my usual six p.m. arrival, key in hand, ready to barge in and catch them in the act. I could hardly still my breath. It was quiet inside; no TV, no stereo. I was struck by the possibility that there would be nobody home; the ramifications of that, as far as Baby Pippa was concerned, were too horrible to contemplate.

There was a distinct probability that things could get violent, depending on how this Francisco guy would behave when confronted. I don't know how long I stood out in the hallway, trying to decide whether I should ring (and give them both a chance to get decent) or simply storm in (and face the consequences). I clutched my cell phone like a weapon, ready to punch 911.

Well, I wasn't going to ring my own doorbell. Whatever they were doing inside would be useful evidence and grounds for dismissal. I would speak clearly and forcefully and the whole unhappy moment would be over in a minute. Okay, here goes nothing, I heard myself mutter. I used my left hand to steady the shaking of my right as I stabbed the key into the lock.

I had expected a burst of movement as Yolanda and Francisco scampered to compose themselves. Instead, Yolanda was holding Baby Pippa in the middle of the room, smiling down at her, humming a little melody, her body swaying from side to side. She looked so neat and proper. The skirt was not as short as I thought, her hair was pulled back rather than gooped and pompadoured. It was all too perfect, as if she'd been expecting me. I sniffed the air for the telltale smells of body fluids, dope smoke and barrio boy cologne. There was only a faint redolence of poop and pee and powder, the good smells of the emerging person that was Baby Pippa.

Then Francisco came out of the kitchen with the formula bottle, pausing to shake a few drops on his wrist. He nodded and murmured a *buenas tardes* at me, but went directly to hand Yolanda the bottle. He gently took Baby Pippa from her while she sat on the sofa and placed a towel over her shoulder to catch the drools and burp-ups.

They glanced toward each other seeming amused at the surprise that must have been written all over my face. Did I think they would be having crazy sex in anticipation of my surprise arrival? Had I hoped this would be the case? You are early, Señor, Yolanda said. This is my novio Francisco. He likes babies and comes to help sometimes.

How to respond? I didn't want to say, Yes I know who you are, fellow. Or what are you doing here anyway? I nodded and tried to live through the moment in as ordinary a social context as possible.

Would you like to take over? She graced me with her smile as she offered the bottle, the spit-up towel, and Baby Pippa to hold in my arms. Then, I watched as she grabbed her backpack from in front of the dead camera lens and pulled Francisco out the door without even waiting for her bus fare. *Hasta mañana*!

> *You can cancel Watch That Nanny at any time. Once your Nanny days are over, simply call us and we'll delete your files and uninstall our hardware. It's been a pleasure serving you. (www.watchthatnanny.com)*

I explained to my wife that I didn't fire Yolanda because she was doing a great job. And no, I wasn't obsessed with her. To prove it, I cancelled the surveillance; for the first time in months, I was able to sleep past my two a.m. anxieties. I didn't have to watch a tape of her antics during the day to suspect that she and Francisco had frolicked in our sheets, splashed around with our soaps and shampoos, cuddled up in our robes. There were telltale signs, and they broke my heart. A whiff of Yolanda's hair on my pillow, a lingering dampness in my towel, a CD still inside the player (Ah, sí, Los Tigres del Norte), and Baby Pippa clearly saying "Yolalah" (her first word?) in her sleep.

In the past few weeks, a new relationship has been established between Yolanda and me. Watching her had become a kind of water-drip torture of the fevered reptilian brain. Now that I've pulled the cameras, she may be better disposed to my adoration. I delight in placing small presents where she will find them: a chocolate on the pillow, a pair of movie tickets inside my robe pocket, a new bar of nice soap in the shower. This thing with Francisco can't last forever. I can be patient. Meanwhile, Yolanda knows that my love for her is true and steadfast. It shows in her eyes when I come home, get a report on Baby Pippa's day, and hand her a ten, or maybe a twenty, for bus fare.

# Three Incidents in the
# Early Life of El Perro

Sleep is impossible in this dark house. Its corners echo with unhappy memories and bitter words. The blistered walls of its damp rooms breathe loss and regret. The Boyhood Home of Presidente Refugio Aguilar had, until recently, fallen into disrepair. Yet, some anonymous friend in the newly reestablished Ministry of Culture has seen fit to appoint me curator of this old house, now a museum, or in the eyes of some, a shrine. The accompanying stipend is a boon for a retired professor, surviving at age seventy-five on a meager pension.

The rooms where I spend my days, though not my nights, are as familiar to me as my own home. Refugio "El Perro" Aguilar was a childhood friend of mine. We were neighbors here in San Dimas. Our mothers became close when they realized their sons had been born within days of each other. They would take us to the park for the mild morning sun. Refugio and I were pushed toward each other as if to encourage a hug or a kiss. He grasped my nose as if he were trying to pull it off, and I cried out in pain and terror. He was my first friend. I was his first victim.

*** 

Growing up, Refugio and I went in separate directions. I enrolled in our provincial university. He went to military college and then to

93

the national law school. He soon entered government service. He was promoted to head the Internal Security Ministry. He was elected president. I taught world literature. We shared a small joke: He chased communists while I kept them between book covers.

Through the years we met sporadically for lunch or coffee, whenever, during his frequent political tours, he made a stop in San Dimas. The call would come unexpectedly. I'd say, "Hola, Perro, qué gusto, how good to hear from you." I was one of the few permitted to call him Perro to his face.

The Aguilar home is typical of the houses of San Dimas, a high wall and a heavy oak door protect the inside from the streets, noisy and dusty during drought, noisy and muddy during the torrential rains in summer. The house is on Calle La Fuente; the black number 12 is the only identification that this is the family home of our late president. At one time, a bronze plaque identified the house, but young delinquents gouged the door or painted the walls with various epithets as fast as I could paint them over. I had to finance these repairs out of my own pocket, because the Ministry of Culture did not assign a budget for the upkeep of the Boyhood Home. The vandalism slowed with the removal of the plaque.

Days can go by without visitors. And still, I must keep to my post from 10 a.m. to 6 p.m. Inhibited from taking even the briefest of catnaps, so desirable for a man my age, I pace about the house to stay awake. Each room opens out into the central courtyard where a fountain burbles delicately to create the illusion of coolness in the hot summer afternoons, its murmur masking the rumble of traffic just outside the massive walls.

When someone rings the bell hoping for a tour, I question them. I aim to discourage the morbid voyeur, the potential defacer and the ideological hooligan. Occasionally, I'll claim that I'm closing early, pleading an overload of work, prior commitments, or the ever-handy frail health.

The few that I admit are in for a revealing experience. I know this house intimately. Refugio and I played in its rooms and patios, grabbed treats from its kitchen, wrestled with our schoolwork over the massive table in the dining room. Some ten years ago Presidente Aguilar stole it from its latest owners under the prerogative of national heritage. It remained locked until after his death when it was established as a museum by the Ministry of Culture. It has been up to me to refurbish its rooms with the objects that would make it once again come alive as the home of our late president. Every detail is important. Nothing has been arbitrarily placed because a corner needed to be filled, because a plant might be decorative here, or some nondescript painting cover a crack in that wall over there. The recreation of history is a highly considered act.

It's part of the magic of objects that over the years they become saturated with their owner's personality and speak with a powerful rhetoric of their own. This is the appeal of the Boyhood Home. Its jumble of ostensibly innocent objects: the lamps and chairs and carved end-tables, the leather-bound books and dark oil paintings of angels and heroes and sunsets at sea, the pots and pans and spoons hanging from hooks in the kitchen, the toilet accessories in the bathroom, ivory-handled brushes and combs, tortoise-shell mirrors, fine silk hand cloths. The brass fixtures and the blue-tiled walls, the carved bedposts and the scrolled headboard, the silk slippers, the lace nightgown--this is the stuff of life; it contains the seeds of memory.

Photographs, now yellowed and faded behind their glass frames, catch the moment with no knowledge of their eventual significance. Dozens of such pictures hang from the walls of this house. This photo of Refugio's sixth birthday shows him at the head of a table surrounded by other children. I have picked myself out, in the middle of the table, looking directly at Refugio, with a smirk on my face, as if he and I were already in cahoots over some planned mischief. The names of the other kids are forgotten.

Unobserved, I'm free to treat the house as my own. For the occasional resting of my legs--a necessity--I like the large leather chair that had been favored by Refugio's father, Señor Augusto Aguilar, after returning from the thriving general store he kept open from eight in the morning until ten at night. I keep this room inaccessible behind a velvet rope supported by two brass stanchions. In this formal parlor, Refugio's mother greeted her guests, served little glasses of coffee liquor topped with cream and plates of petit fours. Refugio's family had some sense of how the truly well-off would conduct a social occasion. Even now the room sparkles with the strategically placed crystal vase, the silver candlesticks, the luminescence of purple velvet upholstery on the love seat, and the crocheted antimacassars on the sofa's arms. At night, the room glows under a golden light from a table lamp with a yellow glass shade like a large, upturned goblet over the bulb. It is one of the small satisfactions as curator of the Boyhood Home that I can simply unfasten the rope and be in forbidden space.

When memories come with particular clarity, I make notes. I record what I remember and speculate about what might have happened after Refugio and I drifted apart. Once an event has happened, the echo of the moment rumbles on, faintly if you will, but relentlessly into the present. Several works have already been published about the Aguilar period. Mine is a personal chronicle of Refugio Aguilar's half century of public life. Unfortunately, the temper of the times is not right for its publication; there is no demand in our country for a balanced view of the Aguilar era.

Lurid exposés and outright fantasies do get published. Anybody with a horror story is an author: Refugio Aguilar personally marched his enemies into mass graves or into exile or madness. He was seen pulling triggers, pushing bodies off airplanes, and presenting pink-skinned infants to the wives of his associates. The market for the bizarre and the fanciful seems inexhaustible. Every victim is guaranteed a best seller without regard to historical truth. El Perro must be slain in print over and over, as if we were afraid he might come back from the dead and sink his teeth into our hearts again.

This character assassination by newly formed consensus does not consider that Refugio Aguilar was the architect of our present state of prosperity: a free-market economy that has put us on a par with progressive developing nations. We have German automobiles, Japanese computers, Korean televisions; there are Argentinean beefsteaks inside our American refrigerators, French wines to pour into our Belgian glassware, even an occasional Marxist, of the purely theoretical stripe, in our universities.

In Presidente Aguilar we must accommodate contradictory personalities. The Don Refugio wearing Saville Row pinstripes, a white shirt of supple Sea Island cotton graced with a tie in blue and gold Eton stripes is a different person from the thirty-year old Captain of Internal Security, dapper in a pleated white guayabera shirt in summer and a suede jacket in winter, dun twill trousers always discretely tucked inside black boots, the one silver spur glinting on the right heel.

People assume he became known as El Perro because of his repressive measures as head of internal security. Or that he earned the name because of his loyalty to his friends. Also, it is said he held on to power with the tenacity of a dog chewing at a bone. The true story of how Refugio became "The Dog" is one of many things that only I know. Inside this gracious house we refer to its most notable inhabitant as Don Refugio or Señor Presidente or General Aguilar or even Tata Fucho as thousands of children were taught to refer to him in school.

***

A woman and her husband came to visit the Boyhood Home recently. She had been living abroad for many years, and now, on her first trip home, was eager to revisit her country's recent history. I should have been somewhat guarded at this explanation. The world is full of people who left at the height of the Aguilar era and are now, after his death, coming back in droves.

The couple was in their forties, the man fairly uninterested and eager to get the tour over with. His wife, on the other hand, moved through the house thoughtfully, pausing in the middle of the silent rooms as if searching out the smell, the look, the sounds of their original inhabitants. She pored over the objects in Refugio's room: his schoolbooks, his student medals, a penknife, a telescope, a book still open to the very page where the reading might have been interrupted. She ran her fingers over everything, as if feeling for dust, or some substance that could not be apprehended by ordinary sight.

She stood at a wall with many photographs, studying each one carefully until she reached the sixth birthday party photo of Refugio and his many guests. Refugio was seated in front of his cake, still unsliced, candles glowing. On his head was a paper crown; the other children wore smaller festive hats.

"That's my mother." The woman put her index finger on the face of a girl seated at the far end of the table, crowded and made small between two large boys. She had her hands on her lap, as if to minimize her presence at the celebration. "She was five," the visitor said to her husband who had been standing nearby, rocking from one foot to the other, breathing an occasional bored sigh.

I took a tentative step toward the couple and made a show of inspecting the photograph, as if her mother's presence at the birthday party were a matter of historical significance. I had a clear recollection of the event, but none whatsoever of the girl she had pointed out. "How very interesting," I said. "We seldom have visitors who have played a historical role in the Boyhood Home."

"I didn't know you had been so well connected." The man winked at his wife.

"It didn't do me any good, now did it," she looked at him meaningfully. "In any case," she added with a glance in my direction, "they didn't get off to a good start, Refugio and Mother."

"Interesting," I encouraged her, always eager to pick up some additional nugget for my book.

"My mother was here that one time along with several children from the school. He bit her."

Her husband chuckled. "He bit your mother?"

"Yes, on the finger." The woman nodded her head vigorously, again including me in her recollection. "It happened just before they were seated at the table for the cutting of the cake, and the photograph, I suppose."

"Why would he bite such a sweet girl as your mother must have been?" He put his arm around her shoulders and gave her a firm squeeze.

"She was tearful to be left alone in this strange house and had been given a lollipop for consolation. This brutish little bully," the woman pointed at Refugio, "bit her finger until she had to let go of the candy. There was blood around his mouth."

"Well, in that sense he didn't change much, did he," the husband laughed out loud, as if he had decided to enjoy himself after all.

"Mother says she remembered screaming at him, and calling him 'perro, perro,' over and over."

"I was there, you know." I pointed at my own face in the picture. "But I remember no such thing. I was at all of Refugio Aguilar's parties, up to his sixteenth birthday. He never bit anyone."

"My mother would not make that up," the woman said. "That is how he got his nickname. Because he would bite people."

"I am not saying your mother was not bitten," I argued politely. "But it was not Refugio Aguilar that bit her."

The woman was angry. Her neck flushed and her hand shook when she reached up to brush a wisp of hair off her forehead. "It's all right, dear," her husband murmured. "It all seems rather trivial now."

"No, Julian," she snapped. "We didn't spend ten years in exile only to come back to the same obfuscation we left behind. El Perro is gone. It's time for the facts, big and small, to come out."

"That is why I am here," I assured her.

"Maybe you do know the truth," she sneered, "but can a friend of his be trusted to tell it?"

"I am a historian, Senora."

99

"So, history is being put in the hands of those that stayed and built careers and lived normal lives, while the rest of us were silenced and tortured and made to vanish. Maybe you can tell me where my brother is. His name is Federico Esparza. Or his wife; her name is Mariana Blasquez. Or their neighbors, Fausto and Hermelinda. Or where their baby girl is."

"I'm truly sorry I can't tell you that," I answered.

"You know nothing?"

"I know how he came to be called El Perro." I shrugged modestly. "In fact, I gave him the name." I knew I had the couple's attention. I yawned and glanced at my watch. "Unfortunately," I said, "it is almost time to close. I'm an old man. This has been a long day."

"It's not so late," the man urged me on.

"In any case," I added curtly, "a story such as the one I could tell you would fall into the category of a special tour."

"A couple of exiles trying to reclaim their history," the man pleaded. "Surely you can sympathize."

"Such private explications are not covered by the basic price of admission," I insisted gently. "Or by my modest salary."

"Ah, but you are a foxy old man," the man laughed, pulling out his wallet and palming it discretely. "Some small gift should make up for the lateness of your closing."

"I cannot accept gifts," I said.

"Julián!" the woman erupted with indignation. "He's just looking for a tip."

"Not a tip, Señora," I said sadly. "As a historian, I expect to be paid for my knowledge."

"So, what is the price of this knowledge you will share?" the man asked, clearly amused now.

"Well, I will tell you how El Perro got his name," I said. "And you will be of the few that know this."

"He'll just make something up," the woman was pulling again at her husband's sleeve.

"Not at all, "I said. "If you don't believe what I tell you, you don't pay me."

"And if we do believe you?" the man asked.

"Then, whatever is your good will," I smiled. "Lo que sea su voluntad."

"But if we don't believe, we don't pay," the woman insisted, with more malice than I thought I deserved.

"Good," I said. "Let us go into the parlor where we'll be comfortable." I took the velvet rope off the stanchion and led my guests into the small sitting room. "This area is reserved for special visitors, you know." I indicated the velvet love seat and the plush taffeta chair.

"Well, it does feel good to sit," the woman sighed.

"I would offer you something," I smiled apologetically.

"That's okay," the man said eagerly leaning forward. "Start."

"I have tried, ever since taking over this responsibility, to vanish forever the nickname of El Perro as it refers to Refugio Aguilar. Ironic, you might say, since I gave him the name in the first place. But that was over seventy years ago, and the original context has been buried under added layers of meaning. Nowadays, El Perro is synonymous with cruelty and greed and power. It's a name that brings out the boogie man, the faceless child-beater, the rapist, the thief of our souls. It languishes behind the screen of dimming memory, the dark furry presence of shame.

"The truth about Refugio and his unfortunate nickname is rather innocent. On our walk to school, Refugio and I would pass a house protected by a vicious guard dog. The dog was kept within a walled patio. At the sound and smell of anyone walking by, it would break into frenzied barking and growling. Refugio liked to stand just outside a wide metal door and convincingly mimic the dog's bark. We thought it was great fun to drive the dog wild. Refugio's mother would beg him not to tease the dog. But even when Refugio obeyed his mother and was silent, the dog would acknowledge his presence with a fierce aria of grunts and snarls and deep moaning growls.

"We passed the house at the same hour every day; the dog would be waiting for us. Sometimes Refugio would start his yapping and woofing from a block away. The dog would be wild with fury by the time we walked by. I could hear it trying to leap onto the street, only to end up slamming itself against the steel door, nails scratching frantically in a futile climbing motion.

"One bright afternoon we were going home from school, and after exacting from Refugio a promise that he wouldn't taunt the dog, our mothers allowed us to run ahead. Two things were odd as we approached the house: The dog was silent and the gate that was normally chained shut was slightly parted. The six-inch gap between the edge of the door and the wall exposed us to a hitherto unseen threat. We stopped abruptly, uncertain now whether to backtrack or rush past the potential danger.

"The dog we had so far only imagined, now stood in our path. It was a lean and angular mongrel. A tremor rippled along the spine beneath its wiry coat. Its jaws were parted to reveal two rows of yellow teeth, a pink tongue hanging mockingly to one side. It blinked past me and focused on Refugio with a jaundiced cloudy gaze, eyes filmed over, the corners crusty.

"I don't know what my friend was thinking at that moment; I was close to tears, in the throes of heartfelt repentance at having enjoyed Refugio's cleverness and the pent-up dog's resulting fury. I could hear our mothers chattering away, ignorant of the confrontation taking place just ahead. I prayed that they hurry to our rescue.

"I imagined Refugio would be feeling similarly helpless. Instead, he took slow, deliberate steps toward the dog. It growled mournfully. There was a tentative recoiling and slight backward shuffling as if to find a more secure footing from which to leap.

"Sensing a momentary hesitation, Refugio seized the initiative. He let out a series of high-pitched barks and growls. He stretched onto his toes and lifted his arms in the air. He jumped about as if possessed by some demon. With every leap the dog was forced to inch backward in order to maintain the original distance. Sensing his advantage, Refugio stepped up the frenzy of his howls and barks, his arms waving, taking those quick small jumps off the balls of his feet. Suddenly, to our amazement, the dog let out a single yelp and scurried back into the house through the narrow opening by the gate.

"By then, our mothers had run to our side. They hovered around us, forming a circle with their arms around our shoulders, their wide skirts billowing and concealing us from the threat. I'm sure his mother's steely grip around his wrist kept Refugio from pressing his advantage and pursuing the dog back inside its own house.

"As the four of us walked calmly along the sidewalk, the dog was silent behind its fence. It still barked at anyone else passing by the house. It continued to be quiet after that day whenever Refugio walked by.

"The next day at school I told everybody about how Refugio made the dangerous dog back down. Refugio was reticent about his own adventure. He could not tell us what he had thought or what he had felt or whether he had been afraid or confident at the moment he exploded in a parody of canine fury. We became a kind of team; he the hero, I the storyteller. With every retelling I raised that moment to higher epic levels. His experience became mine. I started referring to Refugio as El Perro. Even after everyone tired of hearing about it, his feat lived on. When asked by a new kid in school why he was called El Perro, Refugio would shrug with calculated modesty. It was up to me, then, to tell the story. The nickname stuck."

The light outside was waning, and the parlor settled into a lush gloom, the colors of the Persian carpet drawing into its designs the plum and maroon shades of the upholstery, sinking us all into a kind of inner twilight. I enjoyed the silence for several moments. When we finally spoke it was in hushed tones as if afraid to wake the spirits that seemed to hover in the Boyhood Home of Refugio Aguilar.

"You make him sound almost heroic," the woman finally said.

"You expected a monster?" I asked. "He was a normal kid. Full of energy, good humor and resourcefulness."

The man shrugged restlessly, this time pulling out his wallet with a bit of flourish. "How much shall we pay you?"

"You sound disappointed," I said.

"No," he shook his head. "It's a good story."

"But it doesn't explain," the woman hesitated for a moment, "how he became a torturer and a killer."

At this point, I could no longer allow these two visitors to speak disrespectfully of Don Refugio Aguilar. I informed them that it was past closing time, and the visit was over. I herded them through the remaining rooms, turning off lights as we went until they were out of the door.

Then I went back to the parlor. I had accepted the modest gratuity the man had slipped me while his wife was not watching. I closed my eyes, and wondered what I could possibly do with everything I knew, where the lines were drawn from which I could speak or be silent.

Refugio had liked sitting in this chair in his father's absence. I think he enjoyed the position of power the parental throne signified. Tonight, as I sit in the same chair, I get an inkling of what he must have felt.

One day after school I found my friend in this formal room, sprawled in his father's chair, cracking and munching peanuts from a large paper cone. I couldn't help but be impressed with the regal picture he made, engulfed in the massive chair in his starched white shirt, blue shorts, knee socks, his polished black shoes dangling above the floor. He seemed oblivious to everything around him; his small dark eyes and agile fingers fixed on the process of twisting open the peanut and eagerly consuming the inner fruit, chewing with eager smacking sounds even as he rummaged inside the bag for the next victim of his gouging thumbs.

He had been eating peanuts for a long time; the white outer shells and brown papery skins had fallen in a wide semicircle on the rug. He gave me two handfuls of peanuts and I sat on the sofa. Refugio had made a game of cracking them open and tossing the peanuts into his mouth, then placing the shells in the palm of his hand and flicking them with his index finger, trying to see how far into the room he could get them to fly.

We were unusually quiet during the peanut-cracking feast. Our silence must have drawn Refugio's mother to the room. Señora Aguilar was of a sweet and placid disposition, but the mess shocked her into a burst of anger. We (she included both her own disruptive child and his ingenuous partner in crime) had turned her salon into a trash dump.

The room, of course, would have to be cleaned at once by us. She was not about to send their maid, Clara, to do our dirty work. The lesson was that we were responsible for our own mess. I tried to catch her eye, so she would notice the shells bulging out of my pockets. But any overt plea of innocence on my part would be perceived by Refugio as an act of disloyalty. In any case, we had both been convicted.

As soon as Señora Aguilar marched out of the room, however, I realized that Refugio had no intention of participating in the clean-up. By this time he had crumpled up the empty paper bag and tossed it into the sea of peanut shells. In a show of solidarity with his share of the problem, I started gathering shells and scooping them into the bag.

"Let it go," he said. "Mother will do it."

"She said she wouldn't."

"She will. She doesn't have anything else to do," he stated, as if making an obvious point.

I shook my head, not wanting to be part of a confrontation between Refugio and his mother. The quicker the room was cleaned up, the less likely Señora Aguilar's displeasure would follow me to my own home. I was ready to start sweeping up shells, when Refugio addressed me in a terse, unquestionably menacing tone. It was a voice I had not heard before, but which in time would become part of his personality. "Stop, now," he said.

I dropped the shells back on the floor and stood up, uncertain as to what I ought to do next.

"Sit," he said simply. "Back there, on the sofa, where you were."

"I think I should go home."

"No," he said. "We will act like men. We will wait for the women to pick up."

"Your mother thinks otherwise," I pointed out.

"So, what do you think she'll do if we just sit?"

We waited in silence for about twenty minutes. Then, I heard Refugio's mother pass by the salon, sensed the pause in her steps, felt her shadow as she peered into the darkening room. She glared at Refugio and he held her gaze. I could only look down at my shoes. They exchanged not a word. A moment later, Mrs. Aguilar came into the room holding a dustpan in one hand and a whisk in the other. The short-handled broom forced her to stoop; it made her seem very vulnerable. She said nothing until finished. It took her only a moment to sweep the peanut shells off the rug. Then, facing her son in the chair, she simply said, "See? Now it's clean. Clean for when your father comes home."

After she left, I could barely see Refugio's face, but there was enough of a glow from a dim lamp that I could make out a look of triumph in his dark eyes. I slid off the sofa and, without addressing him, and too embarrassed to say goodbye to anyone, skulked out of the house. I was not sure what had happened between Refugio and his mother but,I felt a wave of sorrow for her  and a shadow of remorse, which I have never shaken off.

# Fallen Coconuts and Dead Fish

When Felicia Benthall stepped to the counter to check in for her flight back to Minneapolis from Cancún, the airline guy glanced repeatedly from her to the computer, and then asked where the other passenger was. "You're here. *Pero dónde está tu mamá, Gwendolyn* Benthall?" Felicia started to explain that, as luck would have it, she had no idea. She sneezed suddenly, then waited, mouth open, eyes tearing up, to sneeze again, and after the third time, noisily blew her nose on a wadded-up tissue. Perhaps a shark had eaten her mother, she ventured.

"Seriously," the clerk pleaded, taking a step back.

"Very seriously," Felicia sniffled. The grungy winter cold she'd had in Minneapolis had returned after nearly a week of numbing hotel air-conditioning and searing beach sun. Its symptoms covered the sudden spells of crying that came whenever she thought of her mother. "Join the search for the Missing Mom," she said.

"You're sixteen," the clerk explained with practiced composure as he scrutinized her ID. "This is an international flight," he added. "I could deny you boarding until an adult shows up to take responsibility for you."

"I guess I'm an orphan. Okay?"

Glancing at the line growing behind her, he decided with a sigh that she might as well be someone else's problem and slid the boarding pass across the counter. He stuck Felicia by the lavatories, assigning her the middle seat of row 32, between two people who, from the moment she scrunched in between them, would surely disapprove of her purple hair, a crown-of-thorns tattoo on the shoulder, and a gold hoop dangling from a plucked eyebrow.

Felicia was not an orphan: Even if her mother turned out to be dead, she had a dad waiting in Minneapolis. Beneath her sullen shell, a sadness had been corkscrewing its way into her chest, opening her heart like a cave, chill and damp, with the flutter of bat wings, the smell of decay. She knew that her dad would expect her to explain this odd, unsettling thing that had happened: Two days into the mother-daughter winter getaway, his wife of twenty five years had gone for an afternoon walk along the beach, and not come back.

Felicia now felt responsible. In the months prior to the trip, both parents had gradually lost touch with her. She grew morose. She discovered Vladimir Nabokov and Leonard Cohen. She got her skin pierced, studded and tattooed, her lustrous blonde hair chopped into purple spikes, her good clothes dyed black in the family washer. She had announced her intention to drop out of the eleventh grade and move into a big house in south Minneapolis with other lost children; her mother decided to do something about the situation.

Felicia agreed that, for the duration of the trip at least, her awful behavior would be put on hold. Mother and daughter would become friends again. They would chat into the night like roommates, rub sunscreen on each other, ogle men through big matching sunglasses.

Gwendolyn flirted with the slim brown guys at poolside, and inspired by margaritas, demonstrated disco steps she had learned twenty years before. Felicia tagged along; she took *Pale Fire* everywhere, poring over its puzzling narrative, which distracted her from seeing her mother make an ass of herself. When the same guys that came on to her mom tried to chat up Felicia, she would reluctantly peer up from the page and roll her eyes that they could be such morons. "No gracias, please."

"You'd have fun if you loosened up a bit, honey," her mother urged.

"I am having fun." Felicia held up the book cheerfully.

"We didn't come this far so you could sit in a corner, reading," she scolded gently.

Late on the third day, Felicia realized that her mother had seemed to disappear by stages, as if her physical presence were gradually, in some relentless regression, thinning from the immediate recollection of the day into the stuff of elusive memory. Felicia had expected her back in their room at the Cancún Palace at six p.m. She wavered in her concern. By seven, thoughts of her mom were edged with irritation, but by eight she felt nagging pangs of worry. Texts were going without reply: *WTF where are you?* She was also angry that her mother would behave as if she didn't have a husband back in Minnesota.

\*\*\*

Now, flying home by herself, Felicia was uncertain as to how to clarify this super unclear situation for her dad. He'd demand answers, clues, pictures. None of which she would be able to give him. She anticipated a mean January blizzard and a desolate welcome. He'd be standing solidly before her, his expression dark with melancholy. They would hug before anything was said, his chest and belly buried under the layers of flannel and wool and goose down that he required whenever the temperature dropped below freezing. It would be like being embraced by a bear.

On the night that his wife disappeared, her dad phoned around eight, just as he had called every night. There had been no answer from his wife's phone, so he tried Felicia. He missed his girls, he said. Of course, there were tradeoffs—pizza and beer for breakfast, Tom Petty really loud, and cheap thrills on the web. "How is it going?" he asked. "This mother-daughter thing."

"Great," she said. "Mom's out walking on the beach."

"At night?"

"Oh, it's still light." Felicia lied easily. "We're having a splendid sunset."

"Tell her I called, okay?" he said. "'To say hi. No need to call back, if it's late." She had not heard his vaguely insecure tone before.

Her mother should realize that her unexplained absence had already created problems. She texted again and then scribbled a note on Hilton stationery and placed it on the dresser: *Mom: Where the hell are you??? Daddy called!!!* She was suddenly ravenous in spite of her queasy stomach and heavy mind. She added that she would be waiting in the restaurant.

The Café Playa Bruja had been done up in an air-conditioned Nativity, with neon lights framing a manger under fluorescent palm trees and glowing coconuts. Felicia felt self-conscious sitting alone with a giant piña colada, which she could drink in Mexico without being carded, and a platter of nachos, which she could have all to herself. Close by, the band thumped and blared erratically between salsa and reggae. The leader in a green shirt open to mid-chest, danced around the tables, coaxing people to join the conga line. "No, no, no." Felicia recoiled from the pair of maracas shaking a few inches from her face. "Which part of *no* do you not comprehend?"

By ten thirty, lulled by the sweet rum concoction, and even with no replies to her phone messages, she had convinced herself that her mother would be asleep in her bed. Instead, when she went back, the room with its prints of tropical botanicals, the rattan armchair and headboard, the aqua bedspreads matching the drapes, was glaringly empty. The lights over the bed, in the vestibule, in the bathroom burned brightly, just as she had left them. A jumble of colorful resort clothes lay undisturbed on top of her mom's open suitcase. Felicia's note, crisply folded down the middle, remained exactly where she had placed it, an inch inside the corner of the dresser.

"I'm going out to look for you." The sound of her voice in the empty room startled her. She wasn't sure how she would begin, but she reasoned that her mom walking along the shore did not mean she would necessarily return the same way. It was considered very stupid to be on the beach after dark.

*\*\*\**

"Claro, la señora Gwendolyn!" Enrique at the registration counter remembered her well. He had skin the color of cocoa, long hair sun-bleached in streaks, and a gold tooth which Felicia had admired in spite of finding him as about as captivating as Julio Iglesias. The day before, her mom had found a spot overlooking the garden and had handed Enrique her phone, "Please take my picture, sí?"

"The battery is low," he said. "You can get a disposable camera at the gift shop."

He'd taken several shots of Gwendolyn, coyly languorous by the pool, her lips puckered around the straw as she sipped cocolocos, arms outstretched and breasts raised to the ocean breeze. He said for her to call him Quique. "One remembers such a fun-loving woman." He seemed to be mocking Felicia.

"Have you seen her tonight?" she pressed him. "She had on a green wraparound skirt and a red straw hat."

"Yes, this evening," the man said. "Walking barefoot along the beach, a sandal in each hand."

"Well, she hasn't returned," Felicia said accusingly.

Enrique looked at his watch. "It is early, no?"

"It's almost eleven."

"The clubs close at *four* AM," he laughed.

"You think that's where she is?" She felt suddenly hopeful.

"Of course. Americans go to Baby 'O, to Tropidisco, to Hard Rock."

"That wouldn't be so bad, would it?"

"I myself go dancing every night," Quique added. "Tonight, when I get off work at eleven, I will go to Tropidisco to look for my friends. I will look for your mamá and tell her to call you."

"I'll go with you," Felicia said suddenly. "Another pair of eyes."

The clerk said that yes, it would be better if the señorita went with him. Popular clubs make single men wait in line. Couples are allowed in right away.

"We are not a couple," Felicia said. "We're a search party."

111

At 10:55, Quique left the reception desk and went to change out of his white shirt and Hilton blazer. He came back in a black tank top, leather pants and green lizard-skin boots.

"Won't you be warm in those pants?" She had wanted to add that his tubby physique did not lend itself to the leatherboy look.

"Not so." He grinned at her. "Leather breathes."

From their first stop at Tropidisco she realized that finding her mom would be a matter of chance. Pulsing colored lights barely cut through the smoky darkness to reveal dark bobbing heads and shadowy forms jam-packed in front of the DJ, pressed against the walls, hunkered down at the tiers of banquettes that rose above the dance floor. Quique ordered two margaritas from a waitress in a grass skirt and a top made of two coconut halves.

"I don't want to drink," Felicia yelled loudly over the music.

"We have to buy two cocktails," he said. "It's the rules."

"We're not here to party," she said. "We are looking for my mother, remember?"

"Everybody here is looking for someone. That's what we do in Cancún. Go to clubs and look for our friends."

"Yes, you said that."

"Your mother is a lot more fun than you. You act as if you're the older one."

"Well, excuse me."

When the waitress returned, Quique took both margaritas so Felicia could fish out a credit card. She was not surprised that he expected her to pay. She put the card on the tray, and he handed her the drink.

"I will go search for la señora Gwendolyn," he said. "You can wait in this exact spot, or you can come with me." He walked backwards onto the dance floor. He was reaching out with one hand, holding the drink aloft with the other, dancing his hips from side to side, then, grinning at her, front to back. She turned away until she was sure he was gone.

She leaned against a wall, holding her drink, feeling lost. She tried to make out faces through the gloom. Even if her mom were three feet away, she'd probably miss her. Meanwhile, guys kept trying to coax her onto the dance floor.

"You are waiting for a friend?" one man shouted in her ear.

She nodded her head vigorously.

"Can I keep you company until your friend comes back?"

She shrugged. Her Spanish was limited. She wanted to tell him, "It's a free country, you can stand wherever you want."

He took her silence as yes. "You would like to dance until your friend returns?"

"No, gracias." She shook her head emphatically. "What is it with you people and dancing?" she shouted above the music.

"What is the name of your friend?" he asked in English. "Maybe I know him. I can tell him you are waiting for him all alone in a corner."

"Yes, that would be nice," she shouted. "His name is Quique."

"Ah, sí," he exclaimed. "Quique who works at the Palace?"

"That's the one."

"He is not here any more. I saw him go outside with his friends."

"No, that can't be right. He said for me to wait here. We are looking for my mother."

"Maybe he went to another bar to search."

"No, we just got here. I don't understand what is happening."

"Maybe I can help you," he said. "What does your mother look like?"

"Oh, she's one of a kind." Felicia raised her hands helplessly. "Forty. Blonde. Slutty." She stifled a sob.

The man put his arm around her. He could feel his belly yielding against her. She had not gotten a good look at him, but now he felt large and unwieldy. He smelled of some sweet cologne, his breath moist and boozy on her face. She tried to pull away from him, but his arm was wrapped around her shoulders.

"My name is Federico," he said. "But people like to call me Freddy. I don't mind." He did a lazy shrug. "What are you called?" he asked after a while.

"Felicia," she mumbled.

"Ah sí! *Happy* in Spanish," he grinned.

"Oh, yes," she said.

"But you are not, tonight, so very happy." He contorted his face into a pout.

She pushed him away angrily. "What are you, totally deaf? I've lost my mother." The music had stopped suddenly, and her shout rang loud enough to embarrass Freddy away.

There was a break in the dancing and the DJ's voice boomed throughout the bar announcing the two-for-one margaritas in celebration of someone's birthday. She wove her way through the packed crowd and reached the spot on the dance floor just below the DJ's perch.

"I'm looking for my mother," she called up.

"Oh, qué pena, a lost child," the DJ said sympathetically. "What is the name of your señora mamá?"

"Gwendolyn."

"*Atención*," he called out. "*Güendolín! Güendolín!* Your child is waiting for you!"

An intense spotlight swooped over the heads of the crowd, pointing its bright circle at any American woman who might be the missing Gwendolyn. The crowd picked up a chant, "Güen-do-lín, Güen-do-lín, Güen-do-lín."

"We are having a contest," the DJ announced. "Come to the front señoras and señoritas. La verdadera Güendolín and her daughter will have a happy reunion. The others who are not Güendolín will win a free margarita." Felicia would play along on the chance that her mom might appear.

After much jostling and shoving through the dance floor, half a dozen women, lined up under the DJ's booth. Felicia wondered if they were all women who had run out on their families. The aspiring Gwendolyns were thin and angular, tanned and blonde and brassy, with clunky jewelry and manic makeup. They had the unstrung look of women who sensed time was running out, and were intent on an adventure before closing time, checkout time, boarding time.

Somebody handed Felicia a beer sloshing in a plastic cup. She felt herself being pushed and bumped to a thumping dance beat. She spilled her drink and the wet top clung to her breasts. Blindly, she elbowed her way through the crowd to the club's entrance while new arrivals kept pushing their way inside. From all around her, hands pressed against her thighs, nipped her buttocks, mashed her breasts. Somebody dropped an ice cube down her back and laughed as she wriggled to shake it out.

By the time she stumbled out into the street, she had lost one of her sandals. The smells of bus exhaust and the fishy shore at low tide mingled in the steamy night. The sidewalk outside the club was still crowded with the hopeful awaiting admission, docilely lined up under the watchful eye of two men in flamingo-pink Tropidisco T-shirts. Felicia walked off, limping until she took off the remaining shoe.

\*\*\*

The next morning Felicia awoke to the reality of her mother's absence, now for a whole night, dusk to dawn, so clearly serious. When her phone beeped at eight, she expected it would be her dad. She would have to pick up, just in case it was her mom saying, *Hi, Felicia, I'm all right*. Whatever had happened in the steamy night would be better than this uncertainty. I got lost. I got drunk. I met a wonderful man. I'm starting a new life. Can't wait to tell you all about it.

"I kept calling all night," her dad's voice crackled in her ear. "Where the hell were you?"

"Looking for mom," she said. "I didn't hear the phone. The clubs are noisy."

"She's not back yet?" More angry than concerned.

"Not yet, no," she said. "That's why I was out."

"Where did you look?"

"Everywhere," she snapped. "The street, the hotel lobby, some bar."

"You sound like it's funny."

"Not funny, no," she said.

"I'm coming out there," he said.

"What for? She could be here any minute."

"Don't go to the police," he said. "I hear they're not to be trusted."

"So is everybody else around here." She was thinking of Quique abandoning her when she believed he was helping her. When she called the desk earlier, she was told he had called in sick.

"I'm calling the American consulate," she said decisively. "They'll have some idea of what to do."

"I could fly over this afternoon," he repeated weakly. It was a pointless suggestion. Would they cruise the bars showing pictures of Gwendolyn, put up posters on light posts, tuck flyers under windshield wipers, print her picture on Mexican milk cartons?

"Stay there, dad. If she needs help, you're the one she'll call."

***

Three days later, while the plane bumped around over Texas catching nasty updrafts that threatened to send her diet coke and peanuts sliding down and onto the dozing woman on the adjacent seat, Felicia concentrated on just how she was going to explain her mom's absence to her dad: She had gone out one afternoon and *Poof!* She had left behind a scent of dread and confusion. It was not anything Felicia could put into words, even after spending the remainder of her mother-daughter trip asking questions, waiting for calls, and finally sitting quietly in the dark cool nave of the church.

All around her, old women clicked through rosaries and droned prayers. Stuck inside niches along the walls was a wide choice of potential intermediaries, any one of them more accessible than the official God of Protestants. Here were saints in charge of lost loves, lost causes, lost health, their vestments studded with silver medals in the shapes of body parts. Votive candles served as payment for divine intercession. Felicia bought half a dozen red glasses packed

116

with candle wax. They would be tangible proof of her earnestness. She circled the nave and lit them at the feet of various plaster statues. Her anxiety lifted somewhat.

Once divine intervention had been set in motion, Felicia made an appointment with the U.S. consul, Everett Barrington III. She had to wait a day to see him, because his office, understaffed during the hectic winter season, was simultaneously trying to rescue a couple of American drug buyers in jail, bar brawlers in hospitals, reckless beach walkers and lost children adrift without a peso.

"These situations can always use a little time," the consul had said. Felicia figured that he didn't want to do anything until it was clear that the vanished American citizen had not, in fact, been arrested, kidnapped, hospitalized, or deported. For now, he counseled, she was not to contact the local police, private investigators, emergency hospitals; these would be eager to hustle a gratuity rather than to go on a serious search. The consulate would offer proper advice at the proper time. Meanwhile, a recent photo would be helpful.

Felicia rummaged through her mother's beach bag and triumphantly pulled out the disposable camera from the hotel store. The pictures that Quique had taken would be inside.

The next morning, she picked up the prints from the photo-processing place in the hotel lobby and rushed with the unopened envelope to her appointment with the consul. A search would begin with photos of Gwendolyn as she had looked the day she disappeared. Felicia didn't dwell on the unhappy possibilities raised by the disappearance itself. The important thing was to set wheels in motion. This was the term used by Everett Barrington, who welcomed her with a prolonged hand squeeze and a hard-working smile. He walked to her from behind a big oak desk with the United States flag to one side, and on the wall behind him, a picture of Donald and Melania Trump dedicated to *My good buddy Ev, in fond remembrance of wild New York days.* He took her elbow and steered her to the couch. A box of tissues and a mug of coffee within reach.

"I pictured you older," the man said. "You are obviously a very mature young lady." He couldn't pull his eyes away from the gold ring hanging from her left eyebrow.

"Are you doing anything about my mom?"

"Nothing's been reported to our office," he said. "So she's probably not in jail, in a hospital, or in a morgue."

"That's a good sign?"

"It means that she may have voluntarily disappeared." He added, "More females than males run away in Cancún. Women ditch their husbands, girls run away from home, little old ladies go native in some village. You can live on coconuts falling off trees and fish flopping onto the beach."

"Do many mothers leave their daughters with no money and a hotel bill to pay?"

"What I meant is that living bodies are harder to find than dead ones. Even drownings get washed up on the beach. As soon as the local authorities think they've found an American, we hear from *them*. It's a don't-call-us thing."

She placed the photo packet on the coffee table. "These pictures of mom were taken a couple of days ago."

Barrington raised the envelope flap with his plump white fingers. He looked through the pictures quickly, retaining some as he flipped through the others. He pushed the majority of the photos aside, holding on to half a dozen. "Are these the only ones of your mom?"

"How many do you need?" Felicia sighed impatiently.

"You haven't seen them, have you."

She shook her head. "I picked them up on the way here."

With some deliberation, as if he were dealing a poker hand face up, the consul lay the pictures side by side on the table. "You see," he said, when they were lined up before Felicia. "These aren't really helpful."

The results from the roll in Gwendolyn's camera were so unexpected that Felicia thought that she'd gotten the wrong envelope.

They were all tight close-ups of a woman that was probably Gwendolyn, though her features were not fully revealed. There was a gaping mouth, open at the moment of laughing, revealing a dark cave behind red lips and uneven teeth. The next shot had centered on Gwendolyn's pink tongue. The picture beside it showed only the soft mound of a breast through a wet halter top punctuated by an erect nipple. She couldn't hold her gaze on the others: the toes of Gwendolyn's foot, which she recognized because she had commented on the tacky purple polish; her navel surrounded by the loose skin of her sagging midriff; the V of white panties peeking between her bare thighs.

Felicia was grateful when Barrington swept the photos off the table.

"Is it your mom?"

She struggled to speak through the nausea she felt. "That creep, Quique."

"Quique is a friend?"

"He's a desk clerk. Mom asked him to take pictures. He had the two of us pose together. Others, just Mom by the pool."

"There are no shots of you, that I can see. Just these, of your mother. He should be questioned."

"He hasn't been at the registration desk for three days."

"We'll have someone find him," he said, standing up and smoothing down the front of his wrinkled linen slacks. "But these things take time. Go home, Felicia."

"Back to the hotel?"

"Home."

"What if she's been hurt?" The full weight of the situation seemed to strike her at once.

"We'll definitely call you," Everett promised earnestly. "As soon as we know anything."

\*\*\*

"Okay, are you going to tell me what happened to your mom?" her dad asked once they were in the car, an icy 35W slipping from under them

119

all the way home. He handed her a pack of Kleenex. "Once you pull yourself together."

"Jesus," she sniffed. "It's only a cold. I don't think we should go off and imagine terrible things."

"What kinds of things?"

She did not know what to tell him. "She's probably just having some fling." She tried to make it sound like something that happened all the time in sunny Cancún.

"She would still call," he said with conviction. "She wouldn't leave us to think the worst."

"Even if she doesn't call, they will, for sure."

"Who's they, exactly?"

"The consulate," she snapped. "They're looking for Mom. To either find her and send her home..."

"Or what," he broke into her pause.

"You know, figure out what's happened to her."

"Is that all we're supposed to do?" he said. "Wait for a phone call?"

Felicia had bundled up in the pink tufted parka he had brought for her. It was Gwendolyn's fat down thing with matching snow boots that he'd dug up from a back closet. The big swampy coat made her feel protected, a kid with her dad riding home in a blizzard.

"We could wait for months," he insisted. "Years."

"That's true, Dad," she said. "People can get by forever down there, picking up coconuts and fish from the beach."

He spoke formally to her, as if to seal some arrangement that she hadn't foreseen. "It's going to be just the two of us for now, Felicia." He said her name for the first time, she thought, in years. Since before her purple-hair days. "I hope you're up to the growing up you'll have to do." She kept her eyes fixed straight ahead. The car's headlights hollowed out a white tunnel through the flying snow. She marveled that her dad could see where they were going.

120

# The Relic

The good old days keep popping up from the murk. Last year, I heard from Jeff Calitano who wanted to apologize for terrorizing me in the fourth grade. ("Oh, man, how could I've been such an asshole?") Two months later there was an e-mail from Harriet's high school beau Dermott Norton wanting to catch up with her with news of his divorce, his vasectomy, and his new boat. ("So, *are* you happy?") And so they come, ghosts pinging our computer and phone with confessions, invitations, reminiscences. What fun.

The latest came a week ago. "Hi, guys!" a voice chirped in voice mail. The true sign of a ghost since no one refers to us as *guys* anymore.

"This is someone you knew well, a friend," the woman insisted. "And, guess what? I'm in town." Harriet shot me a look that said that whoever this voice belonged to, it was somehow my fault that we'd been found.

"If you know who I am, call me at 612-347-5697. Messenger from your past. Think Dallas!"

It took Harriet and me just a moment to realize that the voice belonged to Sabrina Mooney.

"Good old Brina. I wonder what she's been up to," Harriet said.

"Call her and find out," I suggested.

"She was more your friend," she countered.

"She wasn't really my friend," I said. "She was Parrish's wife. And the four of us were dope buddies. All I remember is being stoned in the same room with this girl with a big laugh and flashing eyes."

"I know. You thought she was exotic."

"I wonder how she found us," I said. "I don't know where any of those people we knew in Dallas are."

*** 

Harriet and I had pretty good jobs in Dallas, at Big D Business Supply back in 1988. Not interesting but decent, handling the orders and shipping instructions for Big D's line of office products. We were overqualified, of course, with my major in History and Harriet six credits short of her teaching certificate, but in those days, we didn't give much thought to a career.

We moved away for no reason except that Harriet said she was sick of Texans, and just wanted to go someplace where people spoke normal English. Like Kansas City, which is where we ended up.

Our friends at Big D threw us a party at Johnny Bob's Cowboy Lounge to send us on our way. We lost track of most of them except for Sabrina and her husband Parrish Mooney. Brina and Rish they liked to be called. Harriet was sure I'd had the hots for Brina. I said that I would not dignify the accusation with a response. Which totally broke her up.

The four of us listened to the Grateful Dead, went to movies and smoked all the time. Sabrina knew where to buy weed from some acquaintance on the fringe of the Dallas underworld, somebody who'd known George W back then. Those were fine times, but once we lost touch with the Mooneys, we stopped getting high.

We lived about three years in Kansas City, temping at insurance companies processing claims, hanging out with some people we never got to know very well. From there we U-Hauled it with one baby to Oklahoma City where people sounded like Texans again, so we bolted to Seattle and eventually to San Jose with our second kid because there was a good opportunity for me there in data processing. In those years we got one Christmas card from the Mooneys, and later a Xeroxed letter from Sabrina announcing that she and Rish had divorced and that she was moving to San Miguel de Allende in Mexico to be an artist. Not a big surprise, since Brina with her gypsy skirts and jangly jewelry certainly looked like she had artistic inclinations.

After two years in San Jose we moved to St. Paul, Minnesota where we ended up buying an Insty- Prints franchise with money we inherited from Harriet's dad.

"Do we want to call her?" Harriet said.

"We have to," I said. "We were friends."

The next day it was my turn to run the print shop from eight a.m. to three p.m. Then Harriet would be in charge until closing at nine. We'd had the store for a couple of years; by this time, we had expected to build the business up to the point where we could afford to hire someone, so that Harriet and I could have the time occasionally to go to a movie or out for dinner. So far, we were "below expectations."

We flipped a coin to decide who would call the mysterious number. When Harriet came to relieve me, she reported it had been Sabrina Mooney, as we had guessed.

"What is she doing in town?"

"She was short on details, something about business to take care of. With me minding the store until nine tonight, and you working the late half tomorrow, about the only day left to get together is Sunday."

*** 

On Sunday, Sabrina looked just like I expected her to. We couldn't stop staring at each other, Harriet and Sabrina and I, trying to conjure the image of twenty years ago. Her skirt still flowed, her white blouse was cut low to reveal the tops of her suntanned, freckled breasts, her feet appeared cracked and callused in open-toed sandals. Silver jewelry jangled and flashed from her ears, fingers, neck, wrists. She carried a Mexican woven plastic market bag with a Frida Kahlo portrait, the handles hooked on her shoulder, the front of the bag pushed back with her elbow, so that the whole thing rested on her hip. I guessed she was traveling light, and that lumpy, overstuffed bag was it for luggage.

We sat in our deck, which we had screened to keep the mosquitoes out, and sipped iced coffee with Kahlua, at once stimulating and relaxing, if you put enough Kahlua in it.

When I updated Sabrina on our lives, she was not impressed. "I thought you'd be a professor by now," she said. Then, quickly filling the sudden hole, she added, "You guys look great. How do you manage?"

"We're too busy to eat," Harriet said with a tense laugh. "You look the same too. I would have recognized you anywhere."

"I look better than Rish," she sniffed. "He weighs two thirty, his blood pressure is way over the red line, and lumps of cholesterol trudge through his veins like bumper-to-bumper traffic." She let out a victorious cackle.

We were all quiet for a few moments as if in memory of the Parrish that once was and is no more. "It's a good thing I don't need him," she said. "I've been able to do quite well without him, thank you."

"And you're here on business?"

"Sure," she said. "Business. If I can get hold of my client. I've been tracking him down for the past three days. I had a firm order from him, and now he's avoiding me." Sabrina lowered her voice to a conspiratorial tone, "I bet you think I'm dealing drugs. I mean, you should see the look in your faces right now. *Oooops*! you're thinking, *We've invited a dope dealer for Sunday brunch.*" She paused for a moment as if to catch her breath. "It's not like that anymore."

After we ate my signature scrambled eggs with spinach and cream cheese, Sabrina went back to the swinging chair on the deck and fell asleep. She kept the Frida bag close to her all the way through the meal, on her trip to the bathroom, and now beside her while she slumped down on the chair and closed her eyes, snoozing with that trusting, open-mouthed kind of oblivion that children have when they know they are in a safe place. She was out for about an hour while Harriet and I washed the dishes and then sat in front of the television to watch the political talk shows which is one of our favorite entertainments; we don't let much stand in the way of our TV viewing. So even though we were getting kind of nervous about Sabrina just hanging around and sleeping on the porch, we didn't want to wake her.

When she woke up, we had more iced coffee and Kahlua. Then Sabrina took a black jewelry case out of the bag, and, as if it contained something fragile, placed it very gently on the table in front of us.

"And this is the business I'm in," she announced. "Rare things of historical importance. In fact, the object inside that box is worth around seven thousand dollars. I bought if for three some years ago, but once word gets around prices go up like crazy. Now if I could just get hold of Roop, my client," and she pulled out a crumpled slip of paper, and reading from it, said, "that's Rupert E. Kitrell of 1267 Brimhall Boulevard, Wayzata, phone number (925) 338-5844." Her agitation alarmed us a little as she continued, "Then, well then of course, I would have my money and be on my way on tonight's red eye. Mind if I use your phone?"

Harriet and I waited out on the porch while Sabrina called from the kitchen and got voice mail. "Hello, Roop, this is Sabrina Mooney from Mexico. I have the object we corresponded about and would like to show it to you for your consideration. You'll see that it perfectly matches the pic I mailed you a couple of weeks ago. You can reach me here with friends." We heard her give our phone number. Harriet shot me a look as if the whole prospect of ending up with Sabrina staying for longer than we wanted was my fault.

"So, what's this thing that you're trying to sell?" I asked, more to make conversation than out of any real curiosity.

"I'll give you three guesses," she said. "If you guess right, you can keep the thing."

"Keep something that's worth $7,000?"

"Take as many guesses as you want," she grinned.

We must've ventured a dozen different things, from pre-Columbian artifacts to jewelry to a cure for cancer. I tried smelling it, listening to it, placing it on my forehead to sense its psychic energy. "I give up," I said, handing her back the box.

Without a word, she carefully lifted the lid and took out one cotton ball after another until she eventually revealed a curled, brown scrap of something like leather pillowed by satin tufting.

"Don't touch," she said. "It's delicate."

"Seven thousand bucks for a piece of someone's shoe?"

"Look closely now," she said.

"It's an ear, right?" Harriet said. "Jeez, an ear," she repeated.

Something about the curve of the helix, the plump lobe, the neat, translucent cartilage reminded us that the ear had once belonged to a person. Attached to its owner, it had once been a living organ, a sensitive receptor of bird chirps, songs, whispers. It looked like it could hear again, given the proper conditions. At about this point, I saw Harriet beside me shake her head, and slink back into the house. I stared at the thing for several moments and then Sabrina carefully replaced the cotton balls. "It's Juan Diego's ear," she revealed, placing the lid back on.

"Who's Juan Diego?" I asked.

"He was a Chichimecan Indian in the sixteenth century in Mexico."

"Is he a saint or something?"

"Absolutely. That's why the big bucks. The Virgin Mary had a relationship with him. She appeared on a hilltop one day and told him to tell the archbishop that she wanted a church built on that very spot overlooking the Valley of Mexico. He's huge in the Catholic world. A certified saint."

"How did you get this thing?" I asked.

"I have my contacts," Sabrina said. "I've been dealing with relics for some time. Those in the know pay good money for authentic stuff."

"How would anyone know it's authentic?"

"I have a reputation. If I say it's the real thing, serious collectors will accept my word for it. In the past ten years I have bought and sold slivers from the One True Cross, a lock of hair belonging to Saint Theresa, a single strand from the rope that Judas used to hang himself, two prepuces which have been attributed to the baby Jesus. I sold both to one collector, because there was no way to tell which one was the real thing. My cut came to $14,000."

We waited until about ten for the phone to ring, but when it became clear that Roop was not going to call, I offered a ride back to her hotel. She nodded quietly as if she had been expecting a hint that the visit was over, carefully placed the box back inside the straw bag, and wrapped her shawl tightly around herself. "Actually, I've checked out of the room," she said. "I had expected my client to pay me and then I would have been on the midnight flight to DFW."

"I'll take you anywhere you want to go," I offered.

"Actually, I'm kind of broke right now. I have a Visa card and all, but it only works in pesos. And I have my plane ticket of course, but I don't really want to cash it in, since I'm going to need some means of escape in case the Kitrell thing falls through."

"Didn't you have a deal with him?"

"I thought I did. See?" She pulled a folded piece of paper from her bag. "I have a letter from him."

I took the letter and read it. "He says he's not interested, Brina. That he would have to be crazy to pay $7,000 for a mummified ear belonging to God knows who."

I handed her the piece of paper back. She took it and folded it back carefully. "Did you read between the lines?" she insisted. "He's bargaining. That's how this business is run. I'm asking for seven. He might offer five. He knows I'll take six. It's still 60% for me. Not shabby, I would say."

"No, not bad," I repeated.

"I'll give Roop one more chance," she said. "If I can't find him, I'll have to think up a new game plan."

Once Harriet realized the ear was back inside its case she came out on the porch. "Sabrina has checked out of her hotel," I said to her.

"Really?"

"Oh, don't worry about me. I could take the relic over to Rupert's and sleep over at his place. We're friends, you know. We became friends when I met him in Mexico last winter and told him I could find him some good stuff. He was interested."

"Doesn't sound like much of a commitment," I ventured.

"Hey, it's all done with a wink and nudge." She picked up the phone and punched Rupert's number. "Rats, it's voicemail again." Her eyes focused on the distance as if she were picturing Rupert Kitrell standing before her. "I am leaving Juan Diego's ear with my friends." She gave him our name and number again. "I'm flying out tonight. The ear will be in their care, and you can pick it up any time you want to. Just pay them $7,000. Oh, hell, make it $6,000. They'll take cash or check. It was nice knowing you, and doing business with you. Goodbye, Mr. Kitrell. I'm sorry I missed you, but I have a plane to catch."

I could tell Harriet wasn't too excited about being left in charge of the ear. But the thought of getting Sabrina on the redeye, kept her from raising any objections. "I'll make sure this goes into a safe place," Harriet said, holding the black box in both hands.

"Does it need refrigeration or anything special?" I asked.

"A dark closet will be just fine," Sabrina said. "Don't worry, Roop will be calling for it as soon as he gets back from his lake place. I'm sure."

***

Later, driving Sabrina to the airport, she sat close to me and placed a hand on my thigh. "I can't tell you how much I appreciate your help," she said. And the hand felt like a balm on a precise place on my leg that I didn't remember having had touched in months.

"It's fine Sabrina, just a drive to the airport."

"Come on, admit it," she said, her voice going lower to a nice chesty tone. "You were glad to see me."

"Of course I was," I said.

"I mean more than that," she insisted. "I'm the most interesting thing that has happened to you in the last few years. I can tell you were hurting for some excitement."

"Harriet and I have a good life," I said.

"Sure," she laughed. "It's so good you do the same exact thing every day. Even your business involves producing thousands of copies of stuff that's not very interesting in the first place."

Then she gave my thigh a little squeeze and pulled her hand back, and the moment was over. I liked her putting her hand on my leg like that, and if she had done this in the good old days, I would have probably done something reckless even with Parrish being a friend of mine.

But now, at the end of a long Sunday, visions of Sabrina's straw bag full of desiccated organs and mummified appendages was enough to cool any potential passion.

The airport was mostly deserted so I was able to leave the car in a loading zone and walk over to the counter with Sabrina. I didn't feel right leaving her at the curb to find her way to the gate. There was also the smallest worry that she might not get on board at all, and then she would be calling and saying she was stranded, and I would have to make this whole trip over to come and get her. Harriet would be pissed. .

I was not surprised at all when I got home to find that Harriet was not asleep and not happy. It was as if she knew that Sabrina had put her hand on my leg and given it a squeeze and that I had found this very gratifying. I don't know how she knew; Harriet picks up on stuff like that. Not that she said anything; she's too smart for that. "So, what took you so long?"

"It didn't take me long," I said. "I got to the airport and waited until tshe was on board."

"Were you glad to see her go?"

"Yes, I was glad to see her go."

"I thought you liked her," she said. "The way her skirts swirled and brushed against your legs, and the way her boobs kept jiggling above the top of her white blouse."

"Yes, well, it was all very arousing. But she's gone," I said, sitting on the edge of the bed and pulling off my shorts.

"But she's not entirely gone, is she? She left her damn ear."

"That's right," I said. "It's still out on the porch."

"Let it stay on the porch."

"No, someone could steal it. It's worth $7,000."

"I don't think I want it inside the house."

I wasn't going to be able to sleep, knowing that the thing was out there, that when the sun came out the next morning its rays would land on the black box and warm up the ear. I could see it feeling the tiny thousands of photons being sucked in by the black box, going through the cardboard and the cotton balls and then tingling the little ear so that it would open up and want to come out of its box. I pulled my shorts back on and walked out onto the dark porch; it didn't feel right handling a sacred relic while naked.

I stood in the middle of the living room holding the jewelry case as if transfixed by the thing, wanting to put it away, for the night at least, but not being able to find a place. I thought of the refrigerator. Somehow it didn't make the butter and cheese and eggs very appetizing knowing they had been in close proximity with a four-hundred-year-old ear. Other places flashed before my mind in quick succession: Garage shelves (not dignified enough), hallway coat closet (frequent use by strangers who might knock the little box about), bathroom medicine cabinet (too steamy), basement (too depressing).

Finally, I found an opening on the bookshelves in the den, upper rung, between *Finding Riches in Unsuspected Places* and *The Home Handyman's Guide to Fixing Anything*. I moved quietly into the bedroom so as not to wake Harriet; I didn't want to have to tell her where the ear was and to have her say that she didn't think it was the right place.

\*\*\*

Things were peaceful with Harriet for a couple of days; she hadn't asked where the ear was. It was bad enough, one of us knowing that the thing was right there, hanging over us as if ready to pounce, without having the two of us worrying. Things got a little restless when by the third day, we hadn't heard from Sabrina's client, Mr. Kitrell. Harriet suggested we give Sabrina a call and tell her that nothing was happening, and that maybe we could send the ear right back to her.

"I already tried caling her," I said weakly.

"Can we write her?"

"Nope. She mentioned that she was living in San Miguel but she didn't say where."

The next bright idea I got was to look up Rupert Kitrell in the book and just tell him the ear was here, and that we would be glad to deliver it to him.

"We are friends of Sabrina," I said. "And we have this relic for you."

"I really don't know what you're  talking about," the voice at the other end of the line said.

"Don't you know Sabrina Mooney, from Mexico?"

"If she's the woman I met at the Puerto Vallarta airport who was selling these weird things, then I guess I've met her."

"What weird things," I asked.

"Bizarre, religious things. I don't want to go into details."

"Yep, that's Sabrina," I confirmed. "She was just here in the city because she said you were interested in this very special relic. That you wanted to buy it, that all that remained was for you two to settle on a price."

"What is this thing."

131

"Well, it's not an easy thing to describe over the phone. It's part of Juan Diego, a famous holy person from Mexico. It's over four hundred years old, beautifully preserved. It's his ear, actually."

"What?"

"His left ear."

"Let me get this straight." Mr. Kitrell was speaking very calmly now, as if he wanted to make sure that he didn't miss a single detail. "I'm supposed to be interested in buying this?"

"For $7,000."

"Jesus.

"Negotiable. Make it $6,000."

"Tell Miss Mooney that she is nuts. That I don't want to see or hear from her again."

"Sure, that's fine, Mr. Kitrell," I said, not really surprised at his reaction. "Do you know her address. So that we can pass on your message?"

"Who are *you* anyway?" he barked.

"I'd rather not say exactly. We are helping Sabrina out with this transaction."

After the man hung up, I got the feeling that he lumped me right in with the Sabrina Mooney circle. That if he ever wandered into my Insty-Prints store and recognized my voice, well, that would be one less customer for the family business. That is one of the dangers of a small neighborhood operation such as ours. It's really a personal relationship kind of selling. If customers get the feeling that I'm a nut, they just won't do business with me. It's as if by giving me their money, they are bonding with Harriet and me. Tim whatshisname would like to think his customers bond with him when they buy a Mac, but it's nowhere close to being the same thing. So, the matter of The Ear and Sabrina Mooney and Roop had to be our little secret, Harriet's and mine.

I certainly had no fear of Harriet telling anyone. As far as she was concerned the whole business of The Ear was behind us, and the only mention of it came about three weeks after Sabrina's visit when she saw the black box on the top shelf of the bookcase and asked me to find another place for it. But I had already gone through that routine, and when I asked her if she had any suggestions, the only thing she could come up with was the trash can.

"Harriet," I said. "You can't throw it out. It doesn't belong to us."

"We can't just hold it for her forever."

"It's worth a lot of money," I said. "Brina will be back for it."

"Put it where I don't see it, where I won't know where it is, where nobody will bump into it. Please."

I could tell Harriet was starting to get a little edgy over the matter of The Ear. So, I decided to act when she wasn't around; I took it out of the box, tacked it to the wall, driving a pushpin through the uppermost point of the helix, and hung a picture on top of it. The picture covering the ear was a framed poster of a big red bathrobe by Jim Dine. Harriet was happy and I was happy, and I figured the ear was happy because it could just sit there in the dark and go up in value. "Wonderful," she said one evening while we were watching Weeds. "The ear is gone."

"Out of sight, out of mind," I sang.

Still, it's surprising how having something like the ear around the house meant that parts of my life would never be the same again. Certain words would trigger a sharp detailed vision of the wrinkled, brown relic. I couldn't hear the words ear, earful, hear, hearing, listening, deaf, or cauliflower, without glancing at the bathrobe poster on the wall. For months it hung banished from the lives of ordinary people. Sabrina, who was as far as I could tell its only friend in the world, had not written or called since her visit. Its prospective owner, Rupert Kitrell, had fizzled. Harriet would have been quite content to have me toss it in the garbage, or possibly do it herself if she knew where it was.

*** 

In time I realized that I was in fact the only thing standing between the ear and its plunge into obscurity or worse. If I died or lost it, the world would never know it had at one time been worth $7,000, or that it had vibrations dating back over four hundred years. The responsibility was daunting. Occasionally, after I was sure Harriet had fallen sound asleep, I would pad silently to the den, and, standing on a chair, pull down the poster from the shelf. I would sit cross-legged on the carpet and carefully shine a light on the wall to examine it. No matter how many times I pulled down the poster, the shock of the thing was still there, fresh every time I looked at it. Sometimes I could swear it had moved in the time since my last visit and turned a lighter shade of brown, almost translucent, grown some new black fuzz.

Gradually, as my familiarity with the ear increased, I was able to hold it closer to the light, to turn it over on its back, to hold it in my palm feeling its lightness, its warmth, it silky, dry texture. Sometimes I spoke to it. I called it Ear and just talked, half to myself, half in its direction, about some of the things that were going on in my life. Like about how I thought that here I was looking at fifty, and didn't have zip to show for my life, and even my life's companion Harriet seemed to be drifting away, and the kids hardly called anymore, and the idea of thirty more years of just wall to wall, dawn to dusk, week to week inertia was enough to make me want to drink.

"Ear," I would say. "Does my life have any meaning?" And I would wait for a while to see if I could get any kind of an insight, and then I would replace the poster on the wall and go to bed. With any luck Harriet would not know that I had been up at all. And then I'd go to sleep hoping that things would be better in the morning. And they usually were, at least in my own head they were, though I'm not sure the ear had anything to do with this.

But just in case, a couple of nights later, I was sitting at the breakfast table with the ear positioned at the apex of a triangle between a glass of milk and a plate of Oreos.

"Ear," I began tentatively. "Sometimes, the best that life has to offer can be encompassed by a nice bunch of cookies." I'm sure there is some old friend I could call with the news. "Hey there," I would say, "remember me? I won't keep you long."

I didn't realize that Harriet had awakened and come softly down the stairs until I heard her voice directly behind me. "Who in the world are you talking to?"

I turned to face her look of profound disbelief that I would go so far beyond the edges of the rational world in order to be heard.

"Just talking to myself, Harriet," I sought to reassure her. "There's nobody else here, is there?"

# For the Solitary Soul

Welcome ashore. And welcome to the world's most unique cemetery. My name is Bertram Zared. I have been guiding visits such as yours for five years, ever since my contentious exit from NYU's history department. But that is in the past. I have thrown out my old tweed jacket with the leather elbow patches; nowadays, I wear with pride this khaki uniform. Note the creased trousers, the pith helmet, the starched short sleeve shirt. These gold-trimmed epaulets denote my official rank: Visitor Relations Officer. I am known as the honorary mayor of our silent city. You can call me Mayor Bert.

I remind you to maintain decorum in this solemn place. Some of you have come here with a serious purpose, but most have ventured on this tour of our exotic island without knowing what you were in for. I say exotic with confidence, even though it is less than ten miles east of Manhattan. Stay with the group and you will get the most out of your outing before the ferry picks us up in a few hours. Believe me, you will have lots to talk about to the folks back home. Get those phones out! Your pictures on Facebook, Instagram or Reddit will earn you hundreds of "likes." Disposable cameras are also available at the souvenir shop.

The island you are visiting today was not always dedicated to this most quiet and docile of populations. It was a military garrison during the Great War. Around you are the remains of barracks, a mess hall, a gymnasium, and a parade field. The troops housed here were made up entirely of hopeless cowards. It would have been imprudent to throw them into battle and humiliating to send them back to their hometowns. Their mission, they were told, was to protect our easternmost coast from a surprise invasion by sea. In fact, they were being quarantined away from the real battlefronts; one fleeing soldier can infect a whole platoon.

At the end of the war, the battalion of cowards was disbanded, its members scattered to regiments where they would do no harm, behind brooms, mixing bowls, and trombones. The base was abandoned.

A few years later, these same buildings were outfitted to house new immigrants, principally refugees from various European wars. This island, at once near and safely apart from the coast, was a logical stopping-off point for waves of the homeless, the lawless, the stateless, the motherless that have traditionally found their way to our shores. You can no longer hear the babble of their foreign tongues or see remnants of the colorful costumes that clothed their emaciated bodies. But the exotic foods they cooked over makeshift hearths, bubbling in tin cans or sizzling over rusty sheet metal, have left a mark in the sensory patina of our city. Take a moment to sniff the air. You might identify, under the musk of rotting wood and swampy earth, the spices immigrants brought: cumin, asafetida, garlic, and chilies.

I remind you again to stay with the group and not cross the ropes into areas that could prove hazardous. We wouldn't want you to sue us! These wooden buildings have been vacant so long that the roofs have sagged, the walls are rotting, the floor has been reclaimed by mud and weeds. The turning of the seasons has caused the eaves to buckle and the beams to hang by a thread. A sneeze, a sigh or even a funny look could make a column give out and tip over.

This facility was later dedicated to a special kind of mental patient. Being essentially uninhabited, the island provided ideal minimum-security housing for pedophiles, exhibitionists, voyeurs. There was not a child or woman in sight, no boats to the mainland, no privacy for even the most perfunctory act of self-gratification. The gymnasium was perfect for group therapy, where a hundred grown men were marched in for a daily confession of their sins. One by one, they declared themselves the vermin of society, wolves in sheep's clothing, old dogs with no new tricks, bottom--feeders every last one of them. You can read their yearnings scrawled on the crumbling plaster: "Ah, Lo-leee-tah." "*Madame Bovary c'est moi!*" "Where, oh, where, has my baby gone?" For many years this was the pre-eminent facility for the erotically derailed; the cure rate was exceptional with recidivism at less than 23%. The place was closed with the advent of Republican administrations.

Because of the proximity to the city, a mere forty minutes via ferry, there was an attempt to turn all this into a medieval pageant with jousters and jugglers and jesters. Opulent banquets, complete with yards of ale, and suckling pigs; jugs of mead were served family-style on the groaning boards of the refurbished dining hall. Roaming dogs under the tables snarled and snapped over scraps and bones tossed by the happy guests. All this for one, all-inclusive admission fee. Well, the effort was too half-hearted. No amount of paint and banners and canned music could hide the creeping entropy of these unhappy rooms.

Our island now numbers over one million inhabitants. Considering our zero birthrate, that is quite a few. Also, as you examine the grid maps you've been provided, note the orderly layout. Disorder and strife and chaos are the province of the living. Remember the original inhabitants of this island--the soldiers, the immigrants, the deviants? Note the graffiti, trash, smells they left behind. Seagulls have been circling overhead for centuries, screaming, diving, dropping their white guano upon the quick and the dead alike. Children think this is funny. Check out the nifty souvenir caps and sun visors on sale at our gift shop.

Now, we make our way down Lethe Road, which is the principal access to the necropolis. How many of you are familiar with that word: necropolis? Let me see some hands. Great, about half of you. For the other half, it means city of the dead from the Greek roots *necro*-death and *polis*-city. How many other modern words can you think of that begin with the prefix necro? Necromancy, necrophobia, necrophilia. Enough said, you are obviously a bright group.

As we approach the first section of our city, you will experience a sense of the prevailing silence. Many of you will begin to whisper, as if afraid of disturbing our inhabitants. This is a natural reaction. While I can't claim that the dead see and hear us, I am not about to say they don't.

We are standing at this moment in the center of our kindergarten. Note the width of the trenches, about thirty-eight inches, to a depth of six feet, sufficient space to stack about six mini-coffins, one on top of the other. The minis are about the size of a shoe box and are used for infants and fully formed stillborns. This is our most anonymous section because so many babies are abandoned or die before being named. The numbers on these white posts identify location, gender, estimated age from minutes to days, and source—hospital, public restroom, dumpster, church door. The code, which has evolved over the years, was known to a very few until we computerized.

For example, this infant's number, #99-6A-8XT, tells us she was a girl, Caucasian, lived for eighteen minutes, left in a taxicab, Midtown. The population of baby boys and baby girls is evenly divided. At one time, there was a suggestion to divide the babies by gender and paint the posts either blue or pink. In the adult section it's a different story: ninety percent of the unknown, the unclaimed, the unwanted are males. We don't know what to make of that. If any of you have a theory, be sure to write it down when you sign the guest book.

Our next section is small in area but large in philosophical implications. As you can see, it's not quite as regular as the infants' or adult sites. And there are no real paths for visitors, only a narrow trail to serve those who work here. In any case, if you follow me single file, you'll be able to tour what some misguided bureaucrat back in the city, far from the actual heart of things, called Section REF, for reasons that I don't wish to anticipate but which will become clear in due time. Underground, beneath the geometric crisscross of paths and depository trenches, is an assemblage of cartons, mason jars and packages wrapped in plastic, all of them more or less buried in independent niches dug to size, as it were. What we have here is a homage to the sanctity of the human body. Nothing is too trivial for a proper burial. There are severed heads inside hat boxes and bowling-ball bags. There are feet (though seldom two together) inside shoe boxes. Hands, whether detached at the wrist or complete with their corresponding arm, are neatly wrapped in plastic. Smaller parts, such as fingers, ears, noses and the occasional penis, are usually received swimming in a jar of formaldehyde.

What we don't accept for burial are internal organs. Gall bladders, livers, eyeballs and such are incinerated downtown. Why isn't a pancreas, so complex and vital to the body's ecology, honored as much as a foot? Surely, to the trained eye, there would be as much individuality to a lung as to a nose. Yet policy is policy. There is a hierarchy in the body parts we honor. A head gets more respect than a hand. A nose has it over an ear. Index over pinkie. Thanks to vigilant records-keeping, a whole leg, foot included, was once disinterred and consolidated with the rest of its body. We are proud of such moments.

Before we move on to the main section of our island city, I feel obliged to offer an explanation. Today, Thursday, is one of our busiest undertaking days because we get the bodies from Queens, which of late has had a rather high incidence of unlamented deaths. Things go in waves in any business. During the Eighties it was the Bronx, in the Fifties Harlem. Now we get more bodies from Queens than anywhere else. I leave that to other professionals to explain.

Our volunteer burial technicians are in the midst of interring (from the Latin *in terra*, meaning in earth). I will ask our crew to step this way and say hello. Don't be shy, fellows. The actual burial process is conducted with the utmost dignity. I insist on it. No joking, pushing, or speculative chattering. Also, I find that when the attire is dignified, so is the behavior. Hence, the clean white coveralls and the white caps (of the type favored by restaurant workers to keep their hair out of the gravy). They also wear rubber knee-boots, double-ply vinyl gloves, and mouth-nose masks. Once they uncover their faces, you see they are regular fellows; they might be your neighbors or bowling partners. And they could be your cell mates, if any of you were imprisoned at Rikers Island. For them, this duty is about as nice as prison jobs get, with plenty of fresh air, sunshine, and that rare commodity in their world, quiet. The men assigned to it have been on good behavior for years. The reward is a lunch of tuna fish sandwiches, hard-boiled eggs and one Jenny Lee cupcake, which they enjoy on the pier, feet dangling above the water: a little freedom picnic while waiting for the ferry to come get us.

We are lucky to be downwind today, so the odors of human dissolution will be masked by marsh ripeness and seagull caca. However, do stand back from the coffins stacked in the waiting area. These are not your fancy sealed rosewood jobs, but $54 fiberboard models which look nice enough with their natural oak laminate, but which are known to leak fluids and gasses.

Come closer and form a circle around our crew so I can make the proper introductions. This is the only chance many of you will have to actually talk and shake hands with real criminals. Meet Lufkin, a lifer from Willmar, Minnesota. Don't let those baby-blues fool you; he set fire to his parents' barn--while they were in it, milking the cows. He can spot our burn victims a mile away, just from the smell of barbecued bone marrow. He always volunteers to take the fryers, as he calls them; he feels it's a way of atoning. He has matured in prison.

Next to him is Benigno, originally from the Philippines. He was a nurse at Bellevue and had a wicked way with a pillow. He was so touched by the suffering of the aged that, in the quiet of the night, he would slip into the geriatric ward and calmly suffocate the terminally hopeless. He was spotted praying over his last victim, and conclusions were drawn about the rash of unexplained coronary occlusions with gaping mouths and bulging eyes. He still defends his actions as Christian charity. His stubbornness has prevented parole despite his fine behavior.

This little wiry guy is our exchange student from Colombia. His name is Telésforo, and we imported him for his activities with the Cali cartel. He supervised the ethnic cleansing of Los Angeles; that is, he went after all drug dealers who were not from his hometown. He is reputed to have ordered the execution of countless Jamaicans, Dominicans, Russians, and many of LA's own South Centralites. He has a beautiful voice and often sings the old romantic songs of his homeland.

Next to him is Phil the Bean Cruncher. He was an accountant for the Luchese family and had more ways of cooking numbers than his mother had pasta recipes. A small joke, which I hope you will forgive. He is our only white-collar criminal, and he is doing hard time because he is reputed to have over a million dollars stashed away for his retirement. He goes free as soon as he turns over the money. [He either buys his freedom now or he buys himself a happy old age in the Caymans. He can wait, he says].

I will let our boys get back to work. They have a full load to deal with before the ferry returns to pick us up. Mingling with the public enriches their lives, but do not give your phone number to these fellows. From prison, they can only call collect. Give them a few minutes, and you will spend too much time and too much money listening to them whine and beg for books, cigarettes and home baked goodies. They are veritable black holes of the heart.

We now reach the point in our visit when emotions are apt to flare up. Some of you may be wondering if a long-missing brother, a disappeared sister, an abandoned child, or a runaway dad have settled on our sad little island. It's nothing to be ashamed of. You live a fine upstanding life; others choose to walk on the wild side.

The adage that every man dies alone is particularly true for our residents. They don't, however, die anonymously; we know who 92%

of them are. No matter how down and out, everybody carries some scrap of identification, an expired drivers license, a drug prescription, a library card, the last letter they received. We identified one old man by the concentration camp number tattooed on his forearm.

I'd like to think we have buried here artists and writers and scientists and street fighters who could've been famous. The great repository of the could've-been-contenders. One man had nothing in his pockets but a key to a Grand Central Station locker. The time had long expired, but the contents had been in locker limbo in order to charge him for storage whenever he tried to claim his stuff. It was a box tightly bound in strapping tape, containing the manuscript of a novel nearly a thousand pages long. It was titled *The Wonder Singer*. Perhaps you've heard of the author--a Mark Lockwood. No?

Another, also a writer of sorts, had a little notebook with every line filled with the same sentence. *I am Patrick Quinn. I am Pat Quinn. I am Paddy...* Over a hundred pages packed with fine spidery handwriting. Forget your name and only God knows who you are.

I'm passing around some postcards. Address them to yourself so we can let you know if a loved one has been located on our island. Feel free to submit as many names as you want, along with their date of birth. If we identify their place within the grid, we'll mail the card and you can bring flowers on your next trip to the Big Apple.

You can also request disinterment to transfer the body to a family plot closer to home. There is a charge for this. Re-burial is not to be entered into casually. Yet about a hundred times a year, our guys here dig up old bodies, replace the cheap coffin with another brand-new but equally cheap box, and then ferry the contents to the transportation company of choice. They don't all carry remains. UPS doesn't. Yellow Line will take anything, for a price.

My next question: Are there any among you today who have a postcard with the location of a loved one? If you do, please come to the front of the group and I'll point you in the right direction. As I said, the identifying numbers are on these white posts at the corner of each plot. They are chronologically coded so if you get a number starting with 00, then you know it is a fresh burial this year. Next to it is section 99 and so forth. You can follow the grid of paths all the way to 69. We figured thirty years would be plenty to identify. After that, our citizens sink into never-never land.

There's no point carrying this kind of baggage indefinitely, is there? I don't need people wanting to look up long-lost great uncles or some of our most famous unwanteds like Barney K. Fulgum, the multiple rapist/throat slasher, or Rhonda "Rah Rah" Bledsoe, one-time queen of the hoboes.

Fine, if we have no volunteers, we can move on to what has become the high point of our visits here. It's a tradition that started more years ago than I can count, where a few of our residents are picked at random and remembered with a flower, a gentle word, a candy bar, a votive candle, a religious stamp, perhaps a prayer to St. Ptolemy, patron saint of grave diggers and undertakers. Any small, touching thing will express your own reverence for the journey we all must make.

I direct you now to our souvenir shop where, according to your preference, you may purchase some offering to lay on the grave dedicated to an unknown, unwanted indigent, the solitary soul, the *anima sola*. So go ahead, and purchase your offering, and then report back to me for your assigned spot on the grid. How about we meet here again in ten minutes? Those of you who already have something to lay at the grave of the eternally solitary can proceed immediately.

I sense reluctance from some of you. There's nothing to it, really. Let's say you are offering a flower. Well, you stand in front of your square, the men preferably with head uncovered, and you try to conjure the image of the deceased in your mind's eye. The best thing is not to try too hard. Simply close your eyes and enjoy the silence of our city. An image will come. Perhaps of a youth with a lopsided grin, or a wizened old woman, her eyes clouded by cataracts, or a red-faced fellow with fine blue veins filigreeing his nose and cheeks. Don't question. Whatever you get is appropriate. Then, with this image in your mind, you may whisper some greeting, a word of encouragement, a wish for peace. Say the words, not just think them. Speaking your thoughts makes them real.

Why is no one moving? All I see is head-scratching and foot-shuffling. Last week's group got into the spirit of things right away. Perhaps they were a more compassionate bunch. They understood loneliness. Is that such a hard concept to empathize with? Where are you people from, anyway? Let's see a show of hands. Minneapolis? Toronto? Scottsdale?

Yes, I see embarrassment. Afraid to act out an emotion publicly, aren't you? The shame of actually communing with the dead. I mean, if your friends and neighbors could see you now, they'd have a good snicker at your expense. Well, I have news for you. It's just us chickens here. And don't worry about word getting out. The guys with the shovels aren't going anywhere. This thing won't work unless we all participate. You will bond, you'll see. It doesn't matter that you don't want to bond with the rest of the group. Nobody wants to bond, until they bond. That's the beauty of bonding.

I am disappointed, I don't mind telling you. We have spent an interesting couple of hours together, and I thought you were an all-right bunch of folks. Had me fooled. How much did you pay for this tour? $24.50? A bargain really. And now that I ask you to do one little thing for me, and for a few of the million unhappy citizens of this place, you recoil back into your selfishness.

You might think that going along with me is optional. And it is, except for one possible snag. There's a two-way radio back in the office. I use it to call over the ferry to come and pick us up, at the end of the tour, at the end of the work shift, preferably before dark. Now, I am in no hurry. And my boys are in no hurry, because they enjoy an evening here more than night lockup. And you are all obviously in no hurry. As you may have guessed by now, I'm not calling the ferry over until everyone has done their duty for the souls of this place. I don't know how long it will take for all of you to get your offerings and say your words of comfort for the solitary soul. But believe me, being in this place after dark is a whole different experience.

# Transfiguration

"You are not like other gringas," the man said.

The woman whose name was Miriam, and who until that moment had been edging into an adventure with her new Mexican friend, struggled to keep from laughing. She turned her head to glance at his face, which was placidly smiling down at her, as guileless as a child's. Clearly, she decided, this guy Carlos didn't realize what a lame thing he'd said.

They had been lying on an iron frame bed with soft whiny springs, naked together for the first time, she supine, he on his side. The room where she improbably found herself had a small table, one wooden chair, and an enormous free-standing wardrobe with Carlos' clothes neatly lined up on wire hangers. The room's single window opened to a view of San Miguel that was spectacularly like Florence. Sitting up on the bed now, she could see distant sloping hills, red tile roofs, a main square surrounded by bay trees, and the cathedral's soaring spires.

She wrapped the thick cotton sheet around herself, enjoying its rough texture on her bare skin. She recognized the ubiquitous scent of the detergent that everyone in Mexico used. In contrast, the man's brown skin with its light glaze of sweat was redolent of tortillas and chilies and beer. She appreciated that, until that awkward moment, they had been in no hurry, that he could lie next to her, quietly touching only her hair with his fine long fingers, brushing her lips as if the barest motion of the first tentative kiss would beg for permission to kiss again.

For now, the opportunity to move into a deeper intimacy had passed. She should have gathered her clothes, her *Hablemos Español* textbook, her plastic-weave bag with the melon, the three bananas, and the one perfect mango. In a matter of seconds she could have pulled on her underpants, her Birkies, and her prudently shapeless dress, all without further conversation. Before he got even one leg into his American jeans, she would've escaped into the street alarmingly far from the familiar center of the town. Yet Miriam stayed, because she wanted to know how she was unlike other American women.

"Just how many American women have you known?" She played along with him. She should have challenged him instead: Tell me how I am different from all the other earnest women in their thirties using their vacation to study Spanish, painting, creative writing, anthropology, history, archeology, cooking, backstrap weaving, pottery and yoga in San Miguel. All in convenient two-week sessions.

Feeling the mood between them change, the man withdrew his fingers from her tight blond ringlets. Cut like a boy's, his friends had observed when they first spotted Miriam sitting in the square. The haircut, her clunky sandals, her sacklike dress, all explained her lack of interest in them; she was probably a lesbian.

She had been drilling herself on the subjunctive when she sensed that the snickers from the adjacent bench concerned her. She ignored the group at first, and then glanced up quickly as if to catch them staring. She liked the innocent, curious look of one man's eyes. She held his gaze coolly. She would wait him out. His friends left and he stayed behind. He was frowning over the English-language newspaper. He moved over to her bench. "Excuse me," he said. "I read this newspaper sometimes to practice my English. Do you know the meaning of this word?" He pointed to the word *fondness* in a headline: Mexicans Develop Fondness for Sushi.

"Do you like sushi?" she asked.

"I have only seen photos," he said. "Japanese food."

"Yes. Raw fish." She laughed when she saw his mouth pucker in distaste. "It says that Mexicans like it."

"Fondness means *like*?"

"Maybe more than like," she explained. "*Affection.*"

"I could say I have a fondness for you?" he boldly stammered.

"No," she said. "It would be a little premature for fondness."

"Later maybe." He indicated with a nod that he understood the difference.

On this trip Miriam had intended to be open to whatever the fates placed in her path. She would find someone with the air of a revolutionary: a poet, an artist, a Zapatista. It turned out that this guy Carlos was a bank teller with management aspirations. Not the stuff of adventure, but she would go along, because he knew where the best chiles rellenos in town were served, and he so earnestly wanted to have dinner with her. She guessed that after a lesson in the proper drinking of tequila shots—squeeze lemon on the tongue, down with a single, resolute toss, lick salt off the hollow between thumb and index—a declaration of fondness might ensue.

Consequently, things had taken this uncomfortable turn. He was clumsy enough that she figured she might be the first American woman he had ever taken to his little room. At twenty-four, this was not a failing he would want to admit, not even to change the course of this moment. He shrugged off the question that continued to linger in the awkward silence between them. "I have known only a few American women," he said, affecting an air of modesty.

She pulled the narrow sheet away from him and covered herself. "How many?" she insisted.

It was in his favor that she was still in bed with him, even with the sheet up to her chin. He looked toward the ceiling as if waiting for the perfect answer. Miriam figured he was either counting, or thinking up some clever Latin-lover bullshit, or searching for some way to change the direction of their conversation. In any case, she was enjoying the small test of wills.

"How many?" she repeated, just as she thought he might be considering a wriggle out of the problem. She was glad she hadn't simply left. Even if her attraction to this particular Mexican guy was waning, the situation had value as part of her education, the fruits of foreign travel, a little cultural anthropology to brighten conversations.

"Ay, Miriam," he sighed.

"Ay, Car-li-tos."

She waited for his answer. She wondered if the local guys kept a tally of the American women they had seduced. If he said eight, she might be amused and wonder whether he was proud or embarrassed. If he said thirty-eight, she would be concerned. At some level, shock would show in her expression. Even if ten years older than him, she'd only slept with six men: five Americans, one Swede, no Mexicans yet.

"*Cuántas gringuitas*, Carlos?"

He shut his eyes tightly, his brow creased as if he were concentrating on some complex calculation. "Mil," he finally said seriously. He raised his hand to correct himself. "Actually," he tried a sheepish grin, "*novecientas noventa y nueve!*"

Okay, she thought to herself, he is not incapable of irony. She decided she still liked him somewhat. But, even though he pleaded with her (*Por favorcito!*), she did not stay.

***

During the next few days she expected to see Carlos behind the counter at the bank, or puzzling over headlines at the news stand, or in the evening with his friends in the square. She sensed he was lurking just beyond the periphery of her vision, his dark eyes watching her. If he liked her as he claimed, he'd find her. He knew where she went for her Spanish class every morning. She ate lunch at the same patio restaurant. In the evening, she would be in the square, surrounded by the noisy grackles hidden in the bay trees. Sometimes she was afraid she'd scared him away. At others, she grew irritated by what she perceived as his malicious game playing.

Halfway into her stay, Minneapolis was suffocating under two feet of snow, her desk at the ad agency was piled high, her phone's voice mail signal frantic, her computer hard drive would be, hour by hour, accumulating much electronic nagging. Meanwhile, she was puzzling out the ontological subtleties of ser and estar, wondering whether soy tonta meant her stupidity was a permanent condition while estoy enamorada signaled that pangs of love would, like the flu, eventually pass. The next chapter in the textbook would clarify her current emotional state in the light of the subjunctive: I could fall in love, if I thought it would make my Mexican experience richer. (Me podría enamorar, si creyera que eso haría de mi estancia en Mexico una experiencia más rica. Huhhh?) She hadn't deliberately come all the way to this beautiful colonial town to walk around blind to soaring church spires and flowered courtyards and burbling fountains. Instead, she speculated how exactly she was different from other American women who had found the brown skin and thick black hair and white calcium-rich teeth of the Mexican guys so damned attractive.

\*\*\*

Carlos finally showed up on Friday while she sat on her favorite bench in front of the cathedral. He said *buenas tardes* and reached out to shake her hand, before sitting close beside her. He had splashed on a sweet aftershave that smelled like the deodorizer popular among the town's taxis. Brut, she guessed. She clasped his hand firmly, and moved away a couple of inches to establish a cool, reserved distance between them. She tried to appear unfazed by his sudden appearance. She would not show that she was pleased, surprised, resentful, relieved or any of the other contradictory emotions that were streaking through her.

"Where have you been?" he said to her, as if their meeting had been the result of an exhaustive search.

"Where have *you* been?" she countered.

"I asked first."

"No way, José. I'm not playing."

"Not José. Carlos, remember?"

"Vaguely."

"Aha, you are angry with me."

"I'll get over it."

He invited Miriam to a soccer game. Two teams from the town, one representing the central market's fruit and vegetable vendors (Los Angeles Verdes) and the other the bus drivers union (Los Diablos Rojos) met at a field by the main road. About a hundred spectators, mostly families, milled about, snacking on fried pork rinds and drinking beer. The chalk lines had been freshly drawn and there was netting to stop the ball beyond the goal posts. The players wore shiny polyester uniforms with both the blue shirts and the red shirts emblazoned with the same brand names—Cerveza Sol, Baterías Eveready and Banco Nacional. Carlos knew about the game because his bank was one of the sponsors. After ten minutes he was ready to leave.

"I want to see someone score, at least," she said.

"It will be very boring," he said. "They will run on the field for an hour and half, up and down, back and forth. See? Like they are doing now."

"So why did you want to come?"

"I am to make sure they have their new shirts on."

"The players?"

"Yes, we give them the money for the shirts. I have to confirm that they have in fact bought new shirts and that the logotype of the bank is prominent."

Miriam saw that the whole world revolved around advertising. No matter where she went, nothing existed unless it was sponsored by some corporate entity. And this guy Carlos was, of all people she wanted to escape on her vacation, a client. "I imagine they are proud to wear the name of an important bank," she said.

Carlos shrugged. "Sometimes they keep their old shirts and use the money to have a big party."

"That's quite a responsibility, checking up on them."

"Yes. The director of the bank is looking for an assistant manager."

"Let's stay a while," she urged. "The guys in the green shirts look like they're winning."

"They are better players because they have time to practice. They get together outside the market and use a melon or a grapefruit as a ball. They are always looking for something to kick around. The bus drivers spend twelve hours a day sitting behind the wheel, stuck in hot traffic, breathing fumes. They don't have the opportunity to improve."

"I like watching their legs," Miriam said, staying close to the action by following the game's progress along the sidelines. The players had increased the tempo of the game. She could hear their labored breathing, their muttered taunts, the heavy sack-like thump of their bodies slamming into one another. They formed tight knots around the ball, their feet dancing up loose dirt, kicking blindly, elbows digging into ribs, spit flying.

Carlos pulled gently at her elbow as if to shift her attention from the game. "You can look at my legs all you want. I will even run for you." He did a cute running-in-place thing.

She remembered that his legs were spindly and a little bowed. "Thank you. That is very kind of you," she said, not looking away from the men running up and down the field.

"I was making a humorous statement."

"Yes, I could tell."

After the Green Angels scored the first goal, Miriam agreed to go back to town with Carlos. He had borrowed an old VW bug, its dented turquoise carapace rattling and clanging over the cobblestones, its tiny engine roaring like a truck, the inside smelling of gasoline. She expected them to blow up. She asked him to let her off in front of her pensión.

"Can I come in?" he asked, stopping the car by the curb.

"No."

"Bueno," he shrugged undaunted. "I can come by later tonight. I will take you to hear mariachis and drink tequila like a real Mexican."

"I think I've had enough excitement for one day, Carlos."

"You don't understand," he went on, somewhat desperately, she thought. "I would like to have a serious talk with you."

"I do understand," she said.

He asked her to come to his family's house for supper the following Sunday. "Come meet my abuelita," Carlos blurted. He promised the evening would be interesting because it was the feast of the Virgin of Guadalupe. She found the offer endearing. He had been raised by his grandmother, Mamá Toña. He hoped that by taking Miriam to meet Mamá Toña, who at eighty carried the full matriarchal weight of the family, he would impress upon the American woman, different from all others, the special regard he had for her.

"No sé, ya veremos," she said. "We'll see." She was flattered.

"I already told my abuelita that you would come for her special supper," he insisted. "She said that an American woman would not understand our traditions."

"Maybe she's right."

"No. I told her you were different."

\*\*\*

Carlos' grandmother could hardly conceal her distrust of his guest, whom she insisted on calling la señorita in spite of the fact that he had twice reminded her, "Se llama Miriam, abuelita."

Mamá Toña stood squarely before a homemade altar with sepia photos of unsmiling ancestors, some in formal portraits, others simple snapshots in plastic holders, and side by side in silver frames, two pictures of dead babies in their ruffled coffins, their eyelids not fully shut, as if a sliver of consciousness had delayed death at least until this first and last photo had been taken. A picture of the Virgin of Guadalupe as she had appeared to a humble peasant back in 1573 was suspended above the silent portraits.

The old woman led a dozen family members in a recitation of the rosary. Her barrel-shaped body rocked in time to the Hail Marys and Our

Fathers punctuated by the clicking of black onyx rosary beads coiled around her stubby fingers. The group murmured their responses dutifully.

*Dios te salve María, bendita entre las mujeres*, chanted Mamá Toña. Gaze upon her if you dare and be swallowed into the mysteries of birth unsoiled by sin, thought Miriam, as the mumbled jumble of the litany fragmented into distinct, separate voices, some efficient and businesslike, others plaintive and devout. Two boys, apparently nephews of Carlos, showed off by yelling out their responses, as if by sheer volume they might push the ritual to a quicker conclusion. Carlos stood protectively beside Miriam, close enough that she could feel his breath on her ear. He recited the prayers, enunciating clearly, perhaps to coach her into joining in. She felt him against her, the back of his hand pressing on her hip. She marveled at how easily he could combine lust with piety.

Miriam stared vaguely toward the ceiling. A sudden sputter from the flickering candles on the altar drew her eyes to the print of the Virgin of Guadalupe. She sought to sharpen the image by squinting but this only made her eyes tear. The details of the looming virgin blurred to a soft oblong, the central human form diffused, while the halo's radiant striations flaring out from the golden crown to her feet, managed by their contrasting luminosity to overshadow the pink center. At the Virgin's feet, a cherub held a crescent that served as a footrest. Or possibly a launching pad, because now the actual virgin seemed to her poised like a rocket, caught at the last possible second before shooting off into the night. On a more mundane level, the effect was of a giant tamal, the traditional cornmeal cake, its covering of corn husk parted to reveal the central treat.

Then, Miriam gasped as the blurry image of the Virgin of Guadalupe gradually transformed itself into an immense vagina. Surrounded by the flaring outer labia, the inner lips tinged in blue, the dark pink vestibule into the womb's inner sanctum, headed by the hooded clitoral button. For centuries, she realized, Mexicans had been worshiping an image ripe with anatomical revelation.

When the rosary was over, and Mamá Toña came to where she and Carlos were standing, she must have sensed that there was some light in her eyes, which came from a combination of things—waiting so long for supper, and the murmur of the praying voices, and Carlos' hand practically on her ass as he grew bolder. Mamá Toña wanted to know whether the Señorita was catholic.

Carlos moved slightly away from Miriam so that he was no longer touching her, though she still felt the warmth from his body. "No," she smiled apologetically.

"*Judía o protestante?*" the old woman wanted to know.

Miriam wondered whether one might be preferable to the other. She figured it was an even split. If she said she was Jewish then she was a descendant of Christ's killers. If she said she was Protestant, then she was a current traitor to the true path. "Worship of the earth goddess," Miriam stated with conviction.

"*Qué es eso?*" The old woman frowned.

"We revere all holy women," Miriam went on. "*Todas las mujeres santas,*" she said. "*Kali, Tonantzin, Guadalupe.*"

Even as the old woman was shaking her head from side to side, Miriam could sense she was losing her interest. Mamá Toña gave her boy a look of pity and turned away.

*** 

They had not agreed on meeting again when they parted the night before. Yet Carlos was not surprised when she knocked at his door; he expected American women to be impulsive. But as soon as he opened his mouth in greeting, he knew that he'd said the wrong thing: "*Hola, Miriam. Sabes?* My *abuelita* thinks you are crazy."

"What kind of a welcome is that?" she said, dropping her plastic weave bag that this time contained a change of underwear, plus woolen socks and a sweater because nights in the mountain town had been chilly.

158

"You made things difficult between me and my family. They couldn't stop talking about you after you left. I had told them you were not like other American women."

"Well, at least I'm not Jewish."

"Yes, that would not have been good. Anything is better than Jewish."

"I should have told your *abuelita* that I was atheist."

"No. That would have been worse than Jewish."

"How about you?" she said. "Do you care what religion I am?"

"No."

"Yes, you do. If I had been Catholic, you wouldn't have been pushing against my ass like you were during the praying."

Carlos shrugged helplessly. "I have a fondness for you."

"So you feel me up, even while the Guadalupe is watching?"

"Please, I don't want to talk about religion," he said.

"I should have told your *abuelita* what you were doing."

"She thinks you are crazy. That would have been a crazy woman talking."

"I should have said, Mamá Toña, your boy is a dirty, dirty man."

He shook his head in mock impatience. "Miriam," he pleaded. "Let's talk about something else." He was sitting on the bed, while she stood before him. He patted a spot on the bed beside him. She looked around the room. She pulled the chair out from the table. She sat facing him with her legs primly together, the hem of her skirt pulled over her knees.

"You started it. You can change the subject."

"Fine, you want to talk about *futbol*?"

"You're making fun of me."

"No."

"I have a fondness for you, Miriam," he said.

"I am fond of you too, Carlos." She sounded unhappy about it.

\*\*\*

Later that night Miriam sat in a café by herself, gazing down at her airline ticket, a strong cappuccino, and a double slice of the only real chocolate cake in the whole of Mexico. She unemotionally took stock of her Mexican adventure:

She had not managed to avoid stupid men.

She had used international roaming minutes to listen to eighteen annoying work messages.

She had not really mastered the subjunctive.

She could no longer say <u>no</u>, <u>no</u>, <u>no</u> to begging children.

On the plus side, she was different from other American women. She could look straight into the eyes of the Virgin of Guadalupe and know that she had been graced with a wondrous revelation. She had tried to tell Carlos all about it.

# Dr. Sybil's House of Confessions

## *Dr. Sybil*

Dr. Sybil does her work in darkness. She draws the drapes, dims the lights and we are as blind as mushrooms. Except for the occasional stifled sob or thumping heart, we might as well be alone. Her methods are a well-protected secret from one group to the next, here at the Institute Terminus, more familiarly known as *The 'Tute*, devoted to the reversal of terminal conditions of the body, the mind and the spirit.

Five of us sit in a semicircle. We are on our own, our outside contact limited to Dr. Sybil's voice and the occasional, shocking, touch of her fingers on our face, too light to qualify as a caress, more like the breeze from a moth's wings or a secret's moist whisper.

But there is no cure without confession. And no confession counts without full candor and repentance, beginning--necessarily--at the beginning, to find that particular juncture when the mind and the body took a wrong turn, perhaps by chance, more likely by design, which eventually led to the current sad, terminal state. Because everything that has an ending, a terminus, must have a start, an iniciatus. A first mistake can be shown conclusively to lead to a whole lifetime of cumulative errors, a heaping up of transgressions leading to the inevitability of a life in shambles.

"Of the five of you, four can be freed. Facing that part of my method," says Dr Sybil, "one of you is a true terminal. There is nothing I can do for you, except to ease your acceptance of a life of reflection and atonement."

A collective sigh of profound melancholy is heard in the dark room.

"Which one won't you cure?" I ask even as I know there will be no answer.

"It could be any of you," Sybil snaps. "It could be you." In spite of the gloomy pronouncement, I grasp at hope. I checked in with writer's block, a constipation of the brain and the heart. Now, with ideas simmering under Dr. Sybil's alchemy, I discover that one of my characters is attempting to take over my life. Poetic, no?

## Charis

A woman speaks for the first time. "My error is of the body not the mind. I am rotten to the marrow. Surely, there is no doubt that I am the terminal."

Ah, I think to myself, Charis has broken the silence. She is only seventeen, an angelic being who has confessed to a decay of her uterus, a bleaching of her blood and a petrifying of her breasts. She thinks the proof of her terminal decay is in her smell; she says she smells of carrion. This is not true. All of us, the members of her group, agreed that Charis smells of lavender and bergamot. Moreover, the whole of her body radiates a kind of translucent health: her cascading tresses, her porcelain skin, her voice, even in plain speech, as melodious as song. Yet, she has confessed, fully, freely, publicly.

"I am terminal as hell," she repeats.

I'm ashamed to say this, but she may have a point. After all, she is, of the five of us, the only one afflicted with a true physical malfunction. She has described the progress of her disease, from the visible lumps to the shriveling of the body, hair falling off in hanks, to the drying of her skin into a crinkly wrapper.

"No," I say. "You are beautiful. You are God's own perfection."

Out of the gloom, she says, "I love you."

Can I say the same words to her? Certainly one year ago when we were first brought together, the five of us for our season of confession and repentance, I could have said I love your hair, Charis. I love your voice. I love the way you eat cherries, one at a time, sensing the movement of your tongue through the exploding red flesh, its caress of the inner fruit, and the final extraction of the pit from between your lips. What is there not to love about you, Charis?

***

"You're a brave girl," I said to her one morning while we were having coffee in the parlor, clearing the table of the domino sets and card decks and monopoly boards that clutter its surface. With no TVs or radios or newspapers or magazines, the residents as they call us, inmates as we think of ourselves, fall into simple games to pass the time. Games and conversation. The rule being, don't say anything you wouldn't want to explain when it was replayed for the group.

The meeting space has been made as homey as an unlimited budget at Ikea can make it. Tourism posters showing Minnesota lakes, Colorado waterfalls, and Arizona canyons make up for the lack of views. Circling the salon are the doors to the five rooms our group occupies. Some of us have placed Welcome mats at the entrance and decorations on the door, including a fall wreath on Charis's room, and on mine a clever door knocker improvised from a computer mouse.

Charis was still fragrant from her shower, dressed now in a shapeless cotton dress, its color a reddish brown that made her nutty tanned skin downright appetizing as if the touch of my tongue running along her forearm to her shoulder would reveal the taste of mana made flesh. Her burnished curls gleamed under the bright sun streaming through the narrow glass slits. The others in our group were either napping (also a great substitute for the lack of information from the outside world, as if dreams might fill that need with the content of the mind's involuntary imaginings) or facing one of the evaluation panels that had become routine for us.

"Pass the milk, please," she said, pointing her chin at the carton between us.

I slid it toward her, and watched as she poured milk into her coffee, turning the black brew to the color of caramel. "Well, you *are*, you know. Brave."

"I'm not sure being brave is what all this is about." She had paused for several moments as if to regain the original sense of our conversation. "I'm confessing to everything."

"Why?"

"I want to be cured." She shook her head impatiently. "Don't you?"

"I guess I go back and forth on that."

"That's because your body is not rotting."

"My mind is."

"Why would you want to live with a rotting mind?"

"It's the only mind I've known," I said. "I've grown attached to it."

"Doesn't it cause you suffering?"

"It's scary." I smiled. "It also causes me great excitement."

"I'm not talking to you anymore."

"Right. I'm dangerous." I opened up the checkers' board. "Red or black?"

## Lenny

There are four others in our group. Not everyone is as forthcoming as Charis, perhaps because her inner state is so physical, so objective. The others seem to have maladies that vary from the totally subjective to Lenny Verdugo whose life in crime is a matter of public record.

Lenny's career goes back to the fourth grade at La Vista Elementary in La Vista, California, a generic hasta la vista kind of place, not Buena or Chula or Bella. Just plain La La La. But everything that La Vista lacked in individuality, Lenny more than made up for in the particulars of his budding criminal genius.

Sallow-skinned and hollow-eyed, Lenny Verdugo, at nearly seven feet has thumbs the size of kielbasas, perfect for gouging an eye or cracking a windpipe. His head, balding since age twenty and now a perfect egg, should be registered and licensed, a serial number tattooed on the forehead. It has butted noses into a hundred splinters, caved in chests, shattered teeth, mashed softer heads like melons.

Even at age ten, he was able to set himself up as a one-kid extorsion operation, shaking down the other boys for their lunch money and the girls for their underpants, which he would pull off and stash in his cubby in a collection that by the time he entered middle school numbered a couple dozen. Even as an adult, it caused him great satisfaction to send unsuspecting sales clerks and waitresses and even his dentist and social worker, home without their panties, embarrassed into making up some story for husbands and boyfriends, yet relieved to have been spared significant physical assault. In a sense, they were grateful that despite his brute strength he would pull off their delicate thongs, bikinis and rumbas with the delicacy of a lover plucking a flower. He had fast reflexes for a guy his size. His hand would flutter up inside a skirt, and the thumb and index would pinch the elastic band and single-handedly slide the item down their legs while with an arm around the waist he gently lifted his victims off their feet. Then, into his pocket, a nod of his head, and a lumbering exit from the scene of the crime. It would all happen so quickly, with hardly any contact with the victim's skin, that some women would not discover what had happened until they went to pee or shower. Nothing brought out the gentle giant in Lenny Luckow like the taste of a pair of frillies.

Lenny's real vocation was in the performance of such low-brow assignments as labor union recruiting, debt collection, sales training, competitive leveraging, divorce negotiations, lap-dancer protection, drunk bouncing, jury persuasion. He made a good living until he was chosen to attend our group. It took two aides and a doctor to get him into the van; he delivered a couple of roundhouse punches until someone emptied a syringe with 5 ccs of demerol right into his carotid artery. He slept for two days, and awoke as a terminal.

A special cocktail of Klonopin, Xanax and Restoril keeps Lenny on a kind of fuzzy cloud nine, allowing the gentle side of his personality to come through. The mighty Lenny Verdugo thinks he's in heaven.

"Do you know what I miss the most?" he asked one night. "The one thing I can't repent of. The thing that will keep me a terminal until the end of my time."

I like Lenny when he's properly sedated. You can converse with him. "The money," I said. "You miss the money, Lenny. At $400 an hour plus expenses, you were charging the top rate for a celebrity fixer. Right up there with Alan Dershowitz, Gerry Spence, Jim Baker."

"Sure." He shrugged modestly. "But it's not the money I miss."

"I suspect you're going to tell me, Lenny. I'm all ears."

"Odd choice of words," he smiled at the distant memory burbling up. "The last guy who said that to me ended up with his ears in my hands. I yanked them off as easily as if I was pulling leaves off a head of lettuce." His eyes stared out in the distance as the past unfolded. "Such a turkey, all alone in his little bookmaking shop. I asked him if he knew what I was doing in his office, after closing hours... 'Do I need to tell you why I'm here, you asshole?' I asked. And he answered, 'Tell me. I'm all ears.' And then I said, just like that, a brilliant kind of spur-of-the-moment-thing, 'Not anymore.' Then I wrenched 'em off."

I'm ashamed to admit that I laughed as I pictured an ear in each of Lenny's hands, the astonished look of the victim, blood welling out the sides of his head like red earmuffs. Lenny had a way with a story.

"That's what you miss. The high of the hit."

"No," he said, a little sadly. He was silent for a moment, staring at the backs of his hands resting on the table, marveling perhaps at the spindly black hairs growing on his fingers and below his knuckles. "I miss the golden moment."

"I see," I murmured, though I did not see at all.

"The golden moment," he stated, as if revealing a cosmic truth.

"I see."

"You fucking don't see," he said, rather too tersely.

"You're right, I don't. Tell me."

"The golden moment, my friend..." He leaned across the table toward me and lowered his voice to a conspiratorial whisper. "Is God's moment. The instant just before I strike, shoot, stab. The earth stops in its spin, and I'm filled with a surge of power, knowing that I can either hold up the raised fist, or smash it down upon some pathetic asshat's head. Karma is in perfect equilibrium."

"You're a mystic, Lenny."

"It's not me. I told you, it's the moment." He sighed unhappily. "And then one day the moment became an hour, the instant stretched to a lifetime. I waited for the feeling to come. And it didn't."

"Then what?"

"I strike anyway. I have no choice."

I wanted to ask him so much more: Did he see a light at the moment of the raised fist? Did he hear music? Did God whisper sweet nothings in his metaphysical ear? But I stayed quiet, being protective of my ears.

## Zoltan

Our conversation was interrupted, as all private conversations among the five of us are, by the arrival of another of the group. Zoltan Lucknow is here because of his state of constant conflict with God. There is a glint in his eyes, a fevered focus on some vision that is as sharp as some crazed hallucination. His wraparound Ray Bans make him the Lone Ranger of the group. This is not some principled philosophical battle that he's waging. The enmity is personal: Grab Him by the beard and twist until He hollers uncle. To his misery, he sees God everywhere, even in places where most religious types don't. According to Zoltan, God is your toothpaste, your motorcycle, your mom, your boss. Zoltan is out to identify and kill God in all his manifestations—symbols, brands, logos, heroes. At different times in his life Zoltan has been linked with attempts to burn the flag right off some of his neighbors' front porches, take a hammer to the logos on automobiles, wreak havoc in supermarket aisles, poison hard drives. He would be happy if the world could reconnect back to the Middle Ages, when there was only one target: God was God and everything else was just stuff. Now, modern society has metastasized God into a rampage of mind-eating cells. Thanks to this relentless evangelism, Mexico has the highest per capita consumption of Coke and Pepsi, after South Africa. Lithuanians will gladly save up and spend a week's salary on a Happy Meal. There are more Marlboro Men in Taipei than in Texas. But enough of lists. Zoltan Lucknow is forty-something but looks at least seventy, stooped and worn and frail from his ongoing battle with the Almighty.

"I'm fucking exhausted by  being treated like a sicko, when I'm only exercising my right to freedom of non-religion," he said, as he settled in between Lenny and me.

It's come up in our sessions that Zoltan believes his threats and actions fall under the guise of protected speech.

"Just my luck," he added with a sidelong glance. "To be stuck in the same class as a mystic and an artiste. One believes in God, the other thinks he is God."

"I don't think I'm God," I was quick to reassure him. "Not for a moment, you know, unless God turns out to be a hesitant, indecisive, confused, erratic, constipated writer."

"Why that's a perfectly adequate description of God from the point of view of his creation. Do your characters believe they are part of a master plan?"

"They would be offended if I told them this."

"Don't," he spat. "I mean there is no question that if God exists, he's a bumbler."

"No question."

"You're not going to stand up for yourself?"

"I'm a puppeteer with tangled strings. A chef without a recipe. A clock without hands. A scriptwriter who's lost control of his movie."

"Lay off the lists, for once."

"Sorry," I mumbled. "I keep thinking that I'll get at something real and true by rattling off alternatives, choices, directions, options, possibilities."

"Do you ever?"

"Yeah, occasionally an idea will rise out of the verbal muck and hit me between the eyes. It's a beautiful thing to behold."

Suddenly I realized that Lenny Verdugo had been listening and grinning a fool's grin, twitching in his chair as if unable to resist some comment bubbling up from the cellar of his mind into the light of our day room. "Bam, bull's eye!"

"You know what I'm talking about, Lenny."

"You bet."

"Words on a roll."

"Plop goes the eyeball."

"The melodious tone."

"Windpipe cracks like a bone."

"Ah, the semicolon."

"Cleaving a head like a melon."

Zoltan pushed his chair back and clasped his hands behind his head. Just the change of his body seemed to throw a wrench in our back-and-forth ping pong of the mind's experience. After months at the 'Tute we're sensitive to nonverbal signals. Yawns, stretches, eyeblinks, sighs and gasps have evolved into a particular lexicon. "How about coffee?" he asked.

The 'Tute is generous that way. Our day room has a bottomless coffeepot, always available to charge us up so we don't lose our edge during the sessions. They bought Starbucks, until Zoltan complained that the little fish-tailed angel everywhere, on the carafe, the mugs, the napkins was a representation of the divine which interfered with his constitutional right not to have God and Government served up in the same helping. They now brew some generic swill from Folgers. I hope Zoltan is pleased with himself. Still, he is a sweet guy for a zealot. He comes back with three mugs between his hands, one black, two with milk.

"You know," he said, leaning back. "I get really tired of our so, so earnest conversations."

"Well, we're supposed to be doing exercises in self-examination," I pointed out, reluctant to remind him that we are in a 24/7 therapeutic situation. "Doctor's orders."

"Where's Charis?"

"Chemo."

## Norah

"Norah?"

"On her phone."

"She's always on the phone."

"Yeah," giggled Lenny. "The queen of talk."

"I thought phones were against the rules," Zoltan said. "I haven't talked to anyone on the outside for weeks."

"In Norah's case, they didn't want to interfere with her livelihood. She talks for a living," I pointed out. "It's like with my writing. I'm free to write as much as I want. But I'd rather be chatting up perverts like Norah."

"I would love to beat someone up, once in a while. Just to stay primed."

"Great idea, Lenny!"

Zoltan seemed preoccupied. "How do they know Norah is not getting news of the outside world?"

"They monitor her chats."

"I'm sure that's enlightening."

"They get material they can use for her cure."

"Yeah," Lenny laughed. "What a cast of characters! Baby Huggo, Van-essa, The Impaler, Bound for Glory."

Zoltan joined in on the laughter. "Don't forget my favorites— Little Willie Weenis, Fuzzy Wuzzy, Tidy Bowl. That last guy takes the cake, so to speak."

"Come on, people." I coaxed us out of our collective giggle fest. "Making fun of each other's condition does not further healing."

"Norah's clients are the ones that need therapy," Lenny pointed out.

"She is more dependent on them, than they are on her," I corrected him. Suddenly, I'm an expert on The Terminal Therapy.

*** 

Norah is our angel of darkness. My pet name for her is Noirah. It is something I keep to myself; there's no point bragging about the serendipitous result of a typo. Noirah is a vision of darkness, from her lustrous black hair down to the tips of her gleaming witch booties. Even her voice has a gloomy mysterious quality, a smooth contralto that reverberates just beneath her fullsome bosom. She can also be downright invisible in the way some women have of not acknowledging the presence of men who might be coming on to them. Noirah does not give any of us the time of day. Conversing with her entails a process of asking direct questions and being grateful that she answers whatever it is she wants to talk about. The truth is, if you want to talk to Noirah about your own needs, her rate is $2.99 per minute, which comes to an hour's session with a barely decent psychiatrist. Since entering the 'Tute, my freelance assignments have dried up; I can't afford Noirah.

"So, Noirah," I say with deliberate cheerfulness. "How goes the battle?"

"What did you call me?"

"Norah," I say with a shit-eating grin. "No-rah."

"Right. She pours herself a cup of coffee, now inky and bitter after simmering in the pot for an hour, and she sits at the table. Not that she would join us if she had a choice, but it's one of our therapy goals that we bond. That is why there is only one table with five chairs in the lounge. Either be a buddy or be lost. Lenny moves his chair a little out of the way; I find it interesting that Norah scares him. Zoltan follows suit with a symbolic nudge of his chair.

"Don't even try to chat me up," she says. "I just gave Baby Huggo an enema." She flutters her hands about as if to cast off whatever remnants of this procedure may still cling to her.

"What can be the attraction of an enema?" sighs Lenny.

"He likes to be clean and fresh when I put on his diaper." She is unusually talkative. "At least a quart up his asshole, then kablooey! There was brown water all over the bathroom. I used at least three towels to dry him, then half a can of baby powder, finally a Pampers the size of half a bedsheet. He wouldn't let me go until he was sleepy. Sweet dreams, mighty boy."

"Well, amazing that it's just talk." I don't know whether I'm flattering or diminishing her talents.

"Nothing is more real than talk," she says, obviously miffed. "Not the words on your page or the thoughts in your head. Talk is real, a live wire from my tongue through his ear into his brain. Ask Baby Huggo. He knows."

"We're almost colleagues in a way. Words, you know."

"Don't flatter yourself, Scribbler."

By this time Zoltan and Lenny are cracking up. They know I'm envious of Norah because she makes more money than I do. She might even have a larger audience.

"Sometimes my characters are more real than life," I try to explain, not so much as boast. "It can be scary."

"You're like God believing his own creation. Fucking delusional," says Zoltan.

The room is quiet as if they all expect me to refute their barbs. I try to distract them by pointing out a fat green fly that has buzzed into our room.

"Where did that beast come from? We're in an airtight building. Not even street smells get inside." The fly sits on the rim of my empty coffee mug. It does its leg rubbing thing and stares at me with its huge buggy eyes.

"Aha, there is a leak in the system."

"It's a spy."

"It's an angel," Norah ventures.

"May I?" Lenny looks at all of us for permission, but finally his glance settles on Zoltan.

"Go ahead, Lenny," he says. "We can't have any angels disturbing our little hell."

It may seem callous to point out that at the moment the alien fly has been obliterated under Lenny's flat palm, something special has happened here. The truth is that watching Lenny in action is mayhem made poetry, the sheer quick beauty of his reflexes, the hand leaping seemingly out of nowhere, and exploding with a bang on the table, is like witnessing the art of a muscle faster than the eye. One minute Lenny's right hand was cupped under his jaw, supporting his head, and the next it was resting on the table, fingers splayed, the sound of its impact still reverberating in the silent room. Then, slowly, the hand lifts and the fly sticking to the palm has turned into a fuzz-and-slime carcass, no more recognizable now than a nose picking. To think that the current smear contains the remnants of a sophisticated, complex system, the beating of a heart, the pumping of a circulatory system, the assimilating of a digestive apparatus. Oh, fly, where is thy buzz? Lenny grabs a tissue and fastidiously wipes the fly's remains from his hand, then crumples it into a wad and tosses it across the room where it lands gracefully in the corner waste basket. "Three points," he grins.

"Fuzz to fuzz," murmurs Zoltan. "As the believers would say."

"Slime to slime," I add.

"What are you feeling at this point?" Norah asks, breaking her own rule against personal topics outside the milieu of her phone service.

"I'm a finely tuned killing organism," says Lenny without a trace of boasting. "Like a racing thoroughbred, I need a run now and then."

Charis comes back from her appointment and our group is complete. She has a way of entering a room that causes everyone in it to draw a breath. Such is the power of beauty, even of the surface kind, not considering that her insides are supposed to be rotting.

"How did it go?" I'm the first to ask.

"Fabulously," she exclaims with her radiant smile. "I think I'm making real progress. You know," she adds, when she sees our collective skepticism cloud our expressions. "I'm admitting to myself that the root cause of my internal decay is in my own character. Toxic emotions have poisoned my insides. Simple, isn't it?"

"That is just so much bull…shit," Norah exclaims. (I love the ways she spaces out the two syllables, so that "bull" and "shit" have equal weight.) "You are being brain…washed." The rest of us nod emphatically.

"Oh, you guys don't really know me," she says. "Not like I know myself. Not like Dr. Sybil knows me."

"We don't know what Sybil knows." I realize I sound more cryptic than I mean to.

"She knows the evil that lurks in the heart," Charis says.

"In the hearts of *men*,' Norah laughs out loud. "Not women. You're a woman.

"Hearts are hearts," Charis says sadly.

"Come now," Lenny says. "You wouldn't hurt a fly."

Zoltan smiles sweetly. "Charis, you are enough to make an atheist believe in angels."

"Even Lucifer was supposed to be beautiful." Charis disguises whatever she's thinking with a thin-lipped smile. "In any case. If I do my mental self-examination diligently, there's a chance I can effect a cure."

"Repent your ways," Zoltan says.

"In so many words," she says sweetly.

"So, it's all between you and your mirror," Norah says.

"Mirror, mirror on the wall, who's the foulest of them all?" I try to toss it off lightly. "I wish I'd written that."

"Be glad you didn't," says Zoltan. "You're in enough trouble as it is with your literary output."

## Little Nestor

He's right, of course. My writing has caused mostly trouble: libel suits, nasty mail from the religious right and the sensitive left, estranged friends and relations, the proliferation of poisons to the body and the environment. In my film scripts I've screwed up people's lives; in my ad writing, I've unloaded everything from nicotine on children to fluorocarbons in the air. The more successful I've been, the more evil I've wrought. Interestingly enough, I got away with all this for twenty years, until my greatest creation, Little Nestor, aka Nasty, Nogood, Nitwit. He's the hero of my dark and disturbing script, *Facelift*, tragically as yet unsold.

Evil scientist Little Nestor figures out a way to steal people's faces while they sleep. The victim wakes up, goes to the bathroom, takes a piss, stands in front of the mirror and sees a face devoid of character and personality, a bland soft-focus version of his original features. There is enough left over from the original, that he is not apt to suspect anything has happened, simply that now the bland exterior matches his own bland soul.

Meanwhile, across town, or around the world, Little Nestor's customer tries on the face, and goes off with a new look, a fresh personality, a clean identity. It's big business among the deformed and disfigured, the delinquent and the gone missing. *Facelift* is one of those movies that is born fully formed in the consciousness of the writer, a rare, once-in-a-career miracle that produces such money-making gems as *The Full Monty, Titanic, The Bridges of Madison County,* and *The Cleansing.* I wrote *Facelift* in a two-month frenzy, and all the time I believed every word.

And what a time it was: the zone, the chi, the tao, all rolled into one continuous state of bliss. Normal meals made me drowsy and mentally sluggish, so I lived on diet colas and handfuls of granola. I was celibate in order to preserve my creative energy. I took catnaps at my desk, feet up, head lolling back over the edge of my ergonomic aviator chair, waking up just as the leg casters began to slide out. After the script was done, I stuffed the pages inside a box and buried them under a pile of old clothes and shoes, building up my courage to try to sell it for production.

From the beginning, there were dreams. Faint, blurry images at first, then every night growing sharper and more detailed, their narratives increasing in complexity. I piled more stuff on the mountain covering the manuscript box: old phone books, dried paint cans, old unread newspapers. Anything to contain the mysterious power of those scenes. Little Nestor, the mad midget scientist of my imaginings, was wearing *my* face. At first I thought I was seeing myself in the dream, that I had somehow incorporated the persona of Little Nestor, that I had so identified with my creation that I didn't know where one left off and other began. That was the rational explanation.

Then, the dreams stopped; Little Nestor became real. Even before I saw him, there were hints of his presence, the silent eddies of someone criss crossing my path, the hints and revelations of some person that was out to haunt me. He seemed to be going everywhere I did, only a few minutes ahead of me. At my favorite café, where I daily stopped for my latte and pumpkin muffin, Iona, the barista, said, "You should've been here ten minutes ago. I just made a latte for your little brother. Or maybe he's older than you, just smaller." She lowered her hand until it was some three feet above the floor. "Know who I mean? A very little guy."

"Little Nestor."

"Your spitting image."

I suddenly felt very much alone. I had a couple of writer pals with whom I would often exchange horror stories about lapsed options and development purgatory. We met at a bar known for its literary clientele: drunks with writing disillusionment.

"One of my characters seems to have left the story he was contained by," I explained. "His name is Little Nestor. He has taken my face, or at least its surface features, and is going around being me."

Little Nestor and I were linked. You kill Little Nestor and you kill part of me. Little Nestor was already getting haircuts with Inky Liz, teeth cleaning with Wacky Wendy, spine cracking with Doctor Joe. Getting Nestor in to see Sybil could not be so hard. The only problem is that it would have to come from Little Nestor directly, because I had not yet located him. I think he sometimes listens in on my phone conversations.

## Dr. Sybil

She stares at the group until we settle down in a semi-circle, gazing attentively at her patient, placid expression. She has on a stiff little brown suit, the skirt way too short for her age, but just right for her nice old-lady legs. We can't wait to get on with the healing process. Oh, how we want to be fixed. She gazes from one face to the other, enjoying the suspense, the tension of the moment before the healing begins. Who will she start with? Oh, pick me, pick me.

And she does.

"Well, let's start with our famed screenwriter Mark Lockwood," she says, smiling at the faces circling her as if seeking consensus. "How goes the writer's block?"

"He's not here," I hear the familiar voice inside my head.

"Who is it that is not here, pray tell?" she asks with resolute forbearance.

"Locoweed is not here," says the voice sharply.

And who is that I'm speaking with?" she asks, flicking on the lights to a bright glare. "I do see Mark Lockwood's face before me."

"When it comes to Locoweed," the voice says. "What you see is not what you get."

"Well, let me hazard a guess," she says. "Is Little Nestor with us for today's session?"

"Oh. Man, you're good!" My hand jerks up to offer Dr. Sybil a high five. Which she ignores.

She explains to the group, barely hiding the lilt of professional hubris in her voice, "The thing is, Mark has been cured of his writer's block. Little Nestor is proof of that. But leave it to Lockwood's peculiar genius to produce a character in serious need of therapy."

Dr. Sybil looks around, focusing her steely blue eyes on each of us in turn. "We've heard from Little Nestor," she announces. "Now, who wishes to go next?"

"Wait!" I hear my own voice piping out in a staccato bleat. "Am I being ignored here? Is not my pain as worthy of healing as anybody else's? Am I the terminal?"

But our doctor has moved on. She dims the lights and we are as blind as fetuses.

# About the Author

George Rabasa was born in Maine and raised in Mexico. He currently divides his time between St Paul and Campeche in the Yucatan peninsula. His collection of short stories, *Glass Houses*, received the Writer's Voice and the Minnesota Book Award. His novel, *Floating Kingdom,* received the Minnesota Book Award. His short fiction has appeared in various literary magazines, such as *Story Quarterly, Glimmer Train, The McGuffin, South Carolina Quarterly, Hayden's Ferry, American Literary Review* and in several anthologies.

Made in the USA
Monee, IL
07 October 2024

66804624R00111